W9-BUO-986

THE INN BETWEEN

THE INN BETWEEN

BY

MARINA COHEN

ILLUSTRATIONS BY

SARAH WATTS

ROARING BROOK PRESS

New York

Published by Roaring Brook Press
Roaring Brook Press is a division of
Holtzbrinck Publishing Holdings Limited Partnership
175 Fifth Avenue, New York, New York 10010
mackids.com

Library of Congress Cataloging-in-Publication Data
Cohen, Marina, 1967– author.
The Inn Between / by Marina Cohen ; illustrations by Sarah Watts.
pages cm
Summary: During a long car trip, best friends Quinn and Kara explore the strange and creepy goings-on at a remote Nevada inn when Kara's family stops for the night.
ISBN 978-1-62672-202-6 (hardcover)
ISBN 978-1-62672-203-3 (e-book)
1. Ghost stories. 2. Haunted hotels—Juvenile fiction. 3. Best friends—Juvenile fiction. 4. Friendship—Juvenile fiction. 5. Horror tales. [1. Ghosts—Fiction. 2. Haunted places—Fiction. 3. Hotels, motels, etc.—Fiction. 4. Best friends—Fiction. 5. Friendship—Fiction. 6. Horror stories.] I. Watts, Sarah (Sarah Lynn), 1986– illustrator. II. Title.
PZ7.1.C64In 2016
813.6—dc23
[Fic]
2015004042

Our books may be purchased in bulk for promotional, educational, or business use. Please contact your local bookseller or the Macmillan Corporate and Premium Sales Department at (800) 221-7945 ext. 5442 or by e-mail at MacmillanSpecialMarkets@macmillan.com.

First edition 2016
Printed in the United States of America by R. R. Donnelley & Sons Company, Harrisonburg, Virginia

1 3 5 7 9 10 8 6 4 2

For John

THE INN BETWEEN

1

THE SOUND WAS FAINT AT FIRST. Quinn had to concentrate hard to hear it. A low, dull hum, like a swarm of bees a million miles away. No one else in the minivan noticed—at least no one said a word—but with each mile that passed, the sound grew louder. Clearer.

Quinn sat beside Kara in the rear seat of the red Caravan. The desert was a whole other planet. Nothing but gravel and rock, spindly creosote, and cacti spreading out on all sides. She imagined hordes of snakes and scorpions crouched under rocks, waiting for darkness before attacking. Good thing they'd be through the Mojave before nightfall.

The knot Quinn had been picking at came loose. She held the bracelet in her hands. It was frayed but strong. Kara had an identical bracelet. She'd made them back in November, the day after everything changed. They'd worn them ever since.

Quinn ran a finger along the intertwining purple and orange pattern. Two colors tightly woven to form a single band. Only now that Kara was moving away, it was like the threads were unraveling. Quinn couldn't let that happen. She reached over and looped her bracelet through Kara's.

"Hey!" said Kara.

"Quit squirming. Help me retie it."

Kara rolled her eyes. Together they managed a loose knot. They made another and pulled the ends tight.

Quinn patted the linked bands. "Forever?"

Kara smiled. "Forever."

Quinn grinned until the corners of her mouth quivered. The thought of Kara moving a thousand miles away stabbed her inside.

She remembered how they'd met on the first day of kindergarten. Quinn was at a table with three other kids. She was coloring a picture of a leaf.

"You're messy," said the boy beside her.

Quinn looked down and saw orange lines streaking outside the bold black border. A moment before, she'd been proud of her work. Now she wanted to hide it. Before she could, a hand reached over and made a few quick strokes with a black crayon. Quinn's coloring was now tucked inside a brand-new border.

The girl with the short black hair looked at Quinn and smiled. They'd been best friends ever since.

"Who's hungry?" asked Mr. Cawston.

"Starving," said Josh. He was twelve—a year older than the girls—but Quinn was just as tall. Kara was a full head shorter.

"You haven't stopped eating since we left Denver," said Mrs. Cawston. "You're like the Grand Canyon."

"More like Area 51," said Kara. "Mysterious and . . . *alien*." She whistled a sci-fi tune.

"What's Area 51?" asked Quinn.

Josh poked his head through the center aisle. "Aliens landed in Roswell, New Mexico, ages ago. It's a big government conspiracy. The military's still holding one captive in Area 51."

Quinn glanced anxiously at the barren landscape. Hills rose and fell like petrified waves. "Weird."

"What's weird," said Kara, "is no one noticed that the alien escaped. And he's sitting right there." She reached over the top of the seat and flicked the back of Josh's head.

"He's definitely strange," said Quinn, giggling.

"I'm not the one wearing boots in the desert," said Josh.

"They're not boots, they're UGGs. All California surfers wear them."

"You don't even surf," said Josh.

Quinn grinned. "Yet."

He swatted her with his tablet. "I may *be* an alien, but at least I don't *look* like one."

"Stop bickering," called Mrs. Cawston from the front. "Or I'll contact the mother ship and have you all beamed up."

Quinn looked at the pale, cloudless sky and sighed. Perhaps that's where all the missing people were. Cruising the galaxy on a ginormous alien spaceship. She twisted a lock of frizzy brown hair.

Josh powered up his tablet. He was reading *The Time Machine*. For the millionth time.

"Do you ever stop reading?" said Quinn.

"You should try it sometime," he sneered.

"I read," said Quinn. When Kara raised her eyebrows she added, "*What?*"

"Ski brochures don't count," said Josh.

Quinn flicked his upper arm and he yelped. Kara laughed.

Quinn wanted to remind them she hadn't skied all last winter. Plus, she really had started reading—Emma's books. She began twisting her hair again.

"I saw a sign a while back," said Mr. Cawston. "There's a diner coming up."

The journey was passing too quickly. The seventeen-hour car ride was supposed to last a lifetime, but in only a few short hours they'd be at Kara's new home in Santa Monica. Quinn had been excited to spend part of summer vacation there. Now all she thought about was going back to Denver to face school alone. She and Kara had tried their best to convince Kara's parents not to move in the first place.

"You'll get low altitude sickness," said Quinn.

"No such thing," said Mr. Cawston. "Only high altitude sickness. People who move to Denver get that because there's seventeen percent less oxygen."

"Exactly," said Kara. "We're used to having seventeen percent less oxygen. So sucking in seventeen percent more will inflate our lungs like balloons. We'll explode." She puffed her cheeks for effect.

"The sand will bother your skin," said Quinn.

"We'll be covered in festering scabs," said Kara. "I'll probably lose an arm to a rogue shark. And Josh'll be attacked by gangs of nasty sea slugs."

Josh, knee-deep in a bowl of rice puffs, waved a dismissive hand. "Sea slugs are herbivores."

"At the very least," said Quinn, "the humidity will make your hair frizzy." She pointed to her own hair as proof.

Kara nodded fiercely. "Yeah, Mom. You'll look like a troll."

"Hey!" snapped Quinn.

Kara grinned sheepishly.

The plan had failed.

Quinn took a deep breath and wriggled her wrist. The bracelet was uncomfortable. Tying them together was silly. She wasn't sure why she'd done it.

The minivan passed a white metal sign, rust melting down its edges and post. It read: *This property has been under claim since 1954. Enter at your own risk.* Behind it was an army-green billboard. The same rusty white metal letters announced: *Norm's Diner. Next exit.*

They left the interstate and bumped along a dirt road. The tires crunched to a halt in front of an old railcar. It sat in the middle of nowhere, like it had detached from a train a thousand years ago and had been gathering dust ever since.

"You can't be serious," said Kara.

Neon-pink tubes ran the length of the car announcing *Norm's Diner.* More tubes flicked on and off. They moved toward an arrow in the center that pointed to the door.

"It's like that show *Diners, Drive-Ins, and Dives,*" said Mr. Cawston.

"Definitely qualifies as a dive," said Mrs. Cawston.

Josh opened the side door. It was as though he'd opened an oven.

"Come on, Min. Let's check it out," said Mr. Cawston.

"Okay, girls," said Mrs. Cawston. She pointed to their linked bracelets. "Aren't you going to free yourselves?"

"Nope," said Kara.

Warmth spread over Quinn like melted butter. She squeezed Kara's hand and then dragged her out of the backseat. A cloud of dust exploded where her boots hit the dirt. It curled up her bare legs toward her jean shorts. Kara practically fell into her, sending more dust curling upward from her purple flip-flops to her yellow miniskirt. The temperature soared.

"If I stay in the sun long enough, Norm can serve *me*," muttered Quinn.

For a moment she stood statue still. Above the diner, the neon lights buzzed and snapped. But beyond that there was something else.

The hum.

2

QUINN COCKED HER HEAD. The sound came from everywhere. And from nowhere.

"What's wrong?" asked Kara.

"Can't you hear it?"

Mrs. Cawston stopped. "Hear what?"

"That noise," said Quinn.

Kara paused for a moment. "Wind turbines. They have farms of them in the desert."

Kara's dad was at the diner door. "Environmental eyesores. Kill thousands of birds a day. The sound can drive you nuts."

Wind turbines, thought Quinn. That was probably it.

Kara's dad opened the diner door. A bell jingled softly. They followed him inside.

A man sat leaning back in a chair, his feet resting on the counter. Gnarly yellow toenails jabbed out from worn Birkenstock sandals. His jeans were shredded at the ends and his faded floral button-down had seen better days. He was reading a newspaper—*Underground Radical.* Quinn zeroed in on the enormous headline and froze. *Missing Brothers.* It had a photo of two boys.

The man lowered the paper. Long silver hair held in place with a tie-dyed headband framed his pockmarked face. "Whad'ya want?"

"I think Norm ran out of flower power," whispered Josh. Mrs. Cawston elbowed him.

"We were hoping for dinner," said Mr. Cawston. "But if you're closed . . ."

"We're open." He pointed to one of the booths lining the front of the car.

Mr. and Mrs. Cawston stared at each other for a moment. Then Josh's stomach rumbled. He shrugged, walked to a booth, and slid into the seat. Kara and Quinn followed.

They forgot they were attached and tried to sit on opposite sides of the table. Kara pulled Quinn off balance and she nearly fell. She grabbed the table and steadied herself.

Josh sniggered. "Tweedle Dee and Tweedle Dumb."

Carefully Quinn maneuvered into the seat across from Josh and slid toward the window. Kara followed. Mr. and Mrs. Cawston sat in the booth directly behind.

The man tossed three menus on the table. He glanced at the linked bracelets, frowned, and swaggered back to the counter, where he dug mismatched cutlery from blue plastic baskets.

"Check it out!" said Josh. "Dry as Desert Ribs. Cactus Quesadillas. Chuckwagon Chicken. And look, Dad! Norm's specialty—the Diablo Burger!"

"Doesn't *diablo* mean devil?" asked Quinn.

"Yeah! It's got pepper Jack cheese, jalapeño rings, and three kinds of hot sauce!"

"Wow," said Quinn. "Eat *that* and you'll meet *el diablo* sooner than you think."

"I'll have the Roadhouse Chili," said Kara. "Er, you don't suppose it's made from roadkill, do you?"

Mr. Cawston waved and the man strolled over with a pad of paper and a pen.

"Two Diablo Burgers," said Josh. As though to avoid confusion he added, "Both for me."

The man shook his head. "No Diablo Burgers."

Josh's face collapsed like an undercooked soufflé. He scrambled for his menu.

“Roadhouse Chili, please,” said Kara.

Norm shook his head again. “Outta chili, too.”

“Taco Salad?” said Quinn. She was met with the same slow shake of the man’s head.

“What *do* you have?” asked Mrs. Cawston, frustration creeping into her tone.

“Grilled cheese,” said the man. Everyone waited for more options, but none came.

“That’s it?” said Josh.

“’Fraid so,” said the man. “Take it or leave it.”

“I’ll take two,” said Josh quickly.

“Make that six,” sighed Mr. Cawston.

“Six orders of grilled cheese,” the man said, scribbling on his pad of paper as though he might forget.

As they waited, Quinn glanced around. A collection of vintage baseball caps hanging on the wall at one end of the railcar caught her attention. On the opposite wall was a black pay phone. She couldn’t remember the last time she’d seen a pay phone.

The man brought the sandwiches. As he passed Quinn her plate, he glanced at her bracelet and scowled.

“Um, Norm?” said Quinn.

He shook his head. “Not Norm.”

“If you’re not Norm, then who’s the diner named after?” asked Kara.

"No one," said the man. "People around here don't speak the names of the dead once they're gone. Not much point in calling a diner a name you eventually can't speak."

"Why don't you?" asked Quinn. "Speak the names?"

"When we die, our spirits linger near the land for several days. Once the soul passes beyond, we give our names back to the desert."

The man-previously-known-as-Norm glanced again at the tied hands, and then walked back toward the counter.

Quinn was curious. She had to know why he seemed so bothered. She waited until everyone had finished eating. Not-Norm returned with the bill and began gathering the plates. Mr. Cawston was busy fishing through his wallet, and Josh and Mrs. Cawston had gone to the bathroom. Quinn motioned at their tied hands. "I guess you think we're weird."

Not-Norm averted his eyes. "Seen weirder."

"We're best friends," said Quinn.

Kara grinned. "Best friends forever."

Not-Norm dropped his chin. "I once dreamed of a two-headed bird. Half the bird was trying to fly, while the other half was bound to the ground."

Quinn looked at Kara, then at their bracelets. She wanted to ask the man more, when Josh interrupted.

"How are Tweedle Dee and Tweedle Dumb gonna go to the bathroom?" He laughed like a drunken mule. *Eeyhah. Eeyhah.*

"I guess we should try to figure it out," said Kara, dragging Quinn out of the booth.

As they left the diner, Quinn glanced over her shoulder. Not-Norm watched from the counter, a shadow draped over his gaunt face.

The day had deepened. They'd stayed too long in the diner. Soon the snakes and scorpions would be slinking out from under their rocks.

As she got into the car, Quinn noticed a lump of mangled fur along the side of the road. Above, black birds circled. Turkey vultures. She recognized them by their ugly red heads. They swooped, digging their hooked beaks into the fleshy feast. One large vulture came up with something dangling from its beak—an eyeball. Grilled cheese churned in Quinn's stomach as she dove into the backseat. The van began to roll.

The hum was louder now, getting louder by the second. It was like the drone of a jet engine pressing against the walls of Quinn's mind.

An eerie twilight swept the landscape and all the browns shimmered gold. Even the air had a strange amber glow. And everything—the road, the hills, the mountains, and the horizon—melted together with no distinguishing lines to tell them apart.

That was probably why no one noticed the light. Light so powerful, so blinding. Heading straight for them.

3

Quinn meets Emma at their usual spot near the office doors. The November sun is already low on the horizon, setting Emma's auburn hair on fire. The buses are lined up and the parking lot's a zoo. A bitter wind shepherds stray clouds. The musky scent of fall is fading into the woolly-wet smell of winter.

Quinn hugs her arms to her chest. Her cheeks glow scarlet, camouflaging her brown freckles. "I have to stay late."

Emma's forehead crinkles. She scrunches the pink knit cap she's holding in her hands. "What'd you do?"

"Doesn't matter," says Quinn, dropping her chin. Her voice is as thin and wispy as the wind. "I just have to stay."

Kids from Quinn's class rush past. They slow down, their gazes lingering on her. They whisper. They're always whispering.

Emma drops her backpack—the orange one with the huge smiley face. It thunks to the green-tiled floor scuffed with a thousand sneaker skids. "What happened?"

Tears burn at the back of Quinn's eyes. Soon she won't be able to keep them from falling. She shrugs. "It's nothing. Don't make a big deal."

Cold seeps through Quinn's pale gray sweatshirt. It chills her skin, sinking deep into the hollow of her bones. She stares at Emma. Perfect Emma.

Kara approaches. She's hurrying to catch her bus.

"Sorry," mutters Quinn.

Kara stops long enough to cast a withering glare. Then she's off—rushing to make her bus.

"I'll call you," says Quinn.

Emma stares. She waits a moment longer. Then she places her cap on her head and picks up her backpack. She slings it over her shoulder, tucks her hands into her pockets, and with one last look turns and walks away.

The sun is fiercely bright. Quinn squints as she watches Emma head through the chaos of the parking lot and onto the sidewalk.

Suddenly, she wants to call Emma back. She wants to yell, Don't go! *but her throat is chalky—she has no voice. A pink cap moves farther and farther away, bobbing and weaving through the crowd, disappearing into the sunset.*

Quinn lunges forward, but something holds her back. The light is too bright. It stings her eyes.

Then all color washes from the world. Emma is nothing but a dark silhouette melting into the bright sunset that wraps itself around her like a silken cloak.

Emma! Come back!

Quinn struggles wildly. Her feet break free, and she plunges face-first into the light. It jabs and scratches at her. She shields her eyes with her hands.

Then everything disappears—the school, the parking lot, the houses, the street—they're all gone now. There's nothing but light.

Piercing.

Blinding.

Light.

4

QUINN'S BODY THUMPED to the left, then to the right. Her hand found Kara's just as the car screeched to a halt, tearing up the gravel on the shoulder of the road. Everyone talked at once.

"What *was* that?" yelled Josh.

"What's going on?" screamed Kara.

"Spencer?"

Mr. Cawston ripped off his seat belt and turned to face the back. "Is everyone okay? Kara? Quinn?"

"What happened?" said Mrs. Cawston.

"I-I don't know," he stammered. "Did you see those lights, Min?"

"What was it?" asked Kara, still squeezing Quinn's hand.

"Aliens," whispered Josh.

Quinn stared out the window. Beyond the reach of the headlights, shadows danced.

Mrs. Cawston let out a deep breath. She adjusted her glasses. "Don't be silly. It was a truck or transport. We've been driving over thirteen hours." She touched her husband's hand. "You need a break, Spence. Let's stop for the night."

Mr. Cawston rubbed his eyes. He sighed and nodded. "I think I saw a sign near Norm's. There's a hotel on the border between Nevada and California. It shouldn't be far." He took another deep breath, slipped the car into gear, and eased back onto the road.

"My mom," said Quinn suddenly. "I should call her."

Mrs. Cawston got out her cell phone and turned it on. The interior of the car glowed blue in the darkness. "Darn. No service."

"My battery died hours ago," said Mr. Cawston. "And I forgot the car charger."

"Great," said Josh. "My tablet's dead, too."

"Don't worry, Quinn," said Mrs. Cawston reassuringly. "When we get to a hotel, we'll charge the phones. You can call then. And *you*," she said, pointing an admonishing finger at Josh, "you can survive a night without aliens."

Josh huffed and tossed the tablet onto the empty seat beside him.

In the back, Kara squeezed Quinn's hand. Quinn winced. A thin dark line circled her wrist. The bracelet had cut into her skin.

"What's wrong?" whispered Kara.

"It's nothing."

Kara eyed the linked bracelets and sighed. "Sooner or later, we're going to have to untie them."

Quinn knew Kara was right, but her words hurt more than the cut. No matter what Quinn did, no matter how hard she tried, she was going to lose Kara.

She began picking at the threads once again. The knot was tighter. She wasn't sure she'd be able to undo it.

They traveled in silence for some time before Quinn noticed something had changed. The hum had stopped. She jiggled a finger in one ear and listened hard, but it was like someone had hit the mute button.

She dug harder into the knotted threads until they came undone. Her hand fell free just as Mr. Cawston slowed the car. He pointed to a huge billboard caught in the headlights.

"That must be it—the hotel between states," said Mr. Cawston.

"ZZZZZ? What kind of an exit is that?" said Quinn.

"Don't you get it?" said Kara. "*ZZZZZ*. As in sleep."

"Clever," said Mrs. Cawston.

Kara's dad hit the gas and the car lurched forward. "A few days before we left I was checking out the map and I saw a road around here called Z-Z-Y-Z-X. You pronounce it *Zizicks*. I looked it up and supposedly some crazy old man named it. Wanted it to be the last word in the dictionary. People still call it *the last place on earth*." He paused to yawn deeply. "Didn't notice any road called Z-Z-Z-Z-Z, though. At least not on the map I was looking at."

"Well," said Kara, "maybe there was an even crazier guy who wanted his place to be the very very last place on earth, so he called it ZZZZZ, pronounced *ZZZZZ*." She buzzed extra long and everyone laughed.

Just then a sign appeared in the distance. It was the blue *Welcome to California* sign with golden letters and matching golden poppies. Right before it was exit ZZZZZ. An arrow pointed to an off-ramp that led behind dark hills of desert gravel.

The minivan bumped and jostled for what seemed like forever. With nothing and no one else in sight, Quinn felt like they were driving on the dark side of the moon.

"I think I saw the same jagged hill three times already," said Kara. "We're driving in circles."

Josh swallowed. "Just like that episode of *Star Trek* where the *Enterprise* is stuck in a rift in the space-time continuum . . ."

"Look! I see it," said Kara.

Quinn stared into the darkness. A tiny light shimmered in the distance.

"That must be the place," said Mrs. Cawston.

As they drew nearer, the silhouette grew brighter and clearer. It was nothing like the boxy roadside motel Quinn had expected. Instead, the hotel, perched high on a hill, looked more like an enormous Victorian mansion, with long, lean windows all alit.

"Cool," said Josh.

The building was a few stories tall. Quinn gazed up at the roof. It was steep, surrounded by what looked like a wrought-iron fence. In the center sat a separate, smaller structure with oval windows. It reminded Quinn of a jeweled crown sitting on top of a majestic head. All the protruding windows were like giant eyes.

The building seemed very old. Quinn couldn't make out the exact color. Perhaps light blue or gray—but it shone nearly white in the darkness.

The minivan left the gravel road and glided onto the circular drive. They pulled under a red canopy that stuck out from the front entrance like a huge velvety tongue.

Kara's dad got out of the car. He said he was going to check at the front desk and see if they had a room available before he parked.

Kara's mom laughed. "You seriously think this place is short on vacancies?"

"You never know," he responded. "Could be a convention going on."

Quinn wondered what sort of convention would take place in a hotel in the middle of the desert. Rattlesnake? Elvis?

Josh slid open his door. "I'm coming with you."

"Me too," said Kara, scrambling after him.

"Come on, Quinn," said Mrs. Cawston. "I'm sure they have a room. I'll get the overnight. Save us some time."

She stepped out of the minivan and Quinn followed her around to the rear. It was filled with boxes and bags—as much stuff as they could cram into it. Mostly clothes but some books and art. The rest of their belongings and furniture had been shipped. Kara's mother retrieved a paisley overnight bag filled with pajamas and toiletries she'd packed just in case.

Quinn hustled to catch up to Kara, who stood waiting at the front of the hotel. She passed flower beds lit with lanterns, where all sorts of exotic plants and shrubs danced in the flickering glow. It was the most green she'd seen since they left Denver.

The entrance door was massive—made of carved oak panels and bound with gold-colored bars. In front of the door stood a tall man with enormous shoulders and charcoal hair. He wore a scarlet velvet jacket with shiny brass buttons and gray pants with a black velvet stripe down each side. His skin glistened in the lantern glow.

"Welcome to Inn Between," he said in a voice as deep and velvety as his jacket. He smiled and swung the heavy door wide.

Quinn observed him as she passed. He stared at her with intense black eyes. They didn't blink.

5

QUINN DIDN'T KNOW what to examine first. Her eyes flitted like a moth from the wine-colored carpet to the grand staircase with its ornate balustrade to the high ceiling where an enormous chandelier rained a thousand glass teardrops.

She breathed deeply. The air was fresh, and a faint aroma lingered—something pleasant and vaguely familiar. Like the special soap Emma used, the one that smelled like cedar and Granny Smith apples. And bluebells.

"Wow," sighed Kara.

"Wow," echoed Quinn, struggling to take it all in.

"It's gorgeous," said Mrs. Cawston.

"Like something out of *The Time Machine*," said Josh.

"Good thing we decided to stop," said Mr. Cawston. "You miss so much if you stay on the interstate."

Chairs were scattered about the lobby, each with its own small table and reading lamp. Only a few people milled about the large space, some in pairs, most on their own. Quinn barely took notice of any, except one—a man sitting behind a spread of newspaper. He wore blue cotton pajamas. Taped to his wrinkled, veiny hand was a plastic tube—the kind an IV drip fitted into. He looked like he belonged in a seniors home or some kind of hospice. Then the grinding of an old elevator snatched her attention.

"Check it out!" Josh made a beeline for the old-fashioned elevator, muttering about how it looked like the *TARDIS* from *Doctor Who*.

The cramped metal cage was moving upward, and through the fancy bars Quinn saw a short, stout woman with a thick mop of curly orange hair. She wore a uniform just like the doorman's. Beside her stood a woman in a pale pink dress. She was missing a shoe.

"Kindly fasten your seat belts and place your tables and chairs in the upright position," said the elevator operator in a squeaky voice.

"This is the most interesting place I've ever seen," said Kara.

"Yeah," said Quinn hesitantly.

"Welcome to Inn Between," said a woman in a chirpy voice. She stood behind the front desk wearing a velvet jacket similar to those of the doorman and the elevator operator. "We've been expecting you."

Quinn bristled. How could they be expected when they didn't have a reservation?

"That's funny," said Kara's mom. She approached the counter and dropped the overnight bag at her feet. "Because we certainly weren't expecting to come here."

To the right of the woman's shoulder Quinn noticed a large brass plaque. In deeply carved letters it announced: *We've been expecting you*. It was the Inn Between's slogan.

The thin, pale woman tucked a strand of mousy brown hair behind her ear and then smiled. "Still, here you are. Now, how can I help you this evening?"

"Have you got two adjoining singles? Or a suite?" asked Mr. Cawston.

"Certainly," she said. "Which would you prefer?"

The woman's smile seemed warm and friendly, but Quinn had a hard time trusting strangers, especially those who appeared excessively pleasant or polite. The name *Persephone* was engraved on the woman's tag, but Quinn decided to give the grinning woman a nickname. *Phony*.

"Two adjoining," said Kara's mother. Then to Kara's dad she said, "I'll stay with the girls."

Quinn leaned over the marble counter as Persephone reached for a dusty, fabric-bound book with the word *Guests* embossed in gold lettering on the faded red cover.

Next she located a fountain pen—the kind that used real ink—and placed it beside the book. On the wall were row upon row of vintage bronze skeleton keys. Each was unique—different sizes with circular patterns, hearts, or crowns on the end. They dangled above tiny oval plaques with numbers. Room numbers, Quinn suspected, though they hung in no particular order.

Quinn had never stayed at a hotel that used real keys. Most had plastic keycards—like credit cards that you slide through a sensor—though her aunt Deirdre had told her about a tiny hotel in Paris she'd once stayed at that still had brass keys attached to enormous key chains shaped like the Eiffel Tower. It would have been great if the Inn Between used giant cacti.

"Do you need to swipe my credit card?" asked Kara's dad, pulling out his wallet and placing it on the counter.

"Not necessary," said Persephone. "Our policy is you pay when you leave."

"But don't you need an imprint? You know, in case we break—or steal—something?" Mrs. Cawston said, laughing.

Persephone shook her head and smiled. "We believe in good old-fashioned trust."

Quinn scanned the counter. Except for a black dial phone, the kind with the receiver still attached to the base with a coiled cord, there was nothing even vaguely resembling technology. No computers. No printer. No photocopier. Old-fashioned didn't even begin to describe the place.

"That's nice," said Kara's mother. "I like that. Not like those large chains."

Persephone opened the red book to a new page. The paper was thick and goose-fat yellow. "Oh, we're a very large chain. In fact, we have hotels all around the world."

"Really?" said Kara's dad. "I've never heard of Inn Between before."

Persephone dipped her pen in a small pot of ink and scrawled the date. "Ah, well. We don't believe in a lot of advertising. Waste of money, really. We're often fully booked without it." She looked up and smiled again. "Name?"

"Cawston," said Kara's dad.

"First?"

"Spencer."

Persephone wrote his name under the date. "And?"

Kara's mother looked confused.

"I'm afraid I need all the names," said Persephone. "Hotel policy."

Quinn looked at Kara and frowned. This hotel sure had strange policies. But Mr. Cawston didn't seem too bothered. He complied, listing everyone beginning with Mrs. Cawston.

The pen glided and curled until all the names were in the book—ending with Quinn Martin. Persephone blew softly over the ink. She closed the book and turned toward the row of keys, retrieving two and handing them to Kara's dad.

"Here we are," she said. "Adjoining rooms. Two queen beds in each. I hope you find these suitable."

The keys looked different, but each had the exact same number engraved on its side—0708. Quinn thought it was strange, but decided it must be because they were adjoining rooms, treated as a single room and therefore with the same lock.

Josh, who had given up on the elevator, hustled toward the counter. "I'm starving."

"I'm afraid the restaurant is closed for the evening," said Persephone, motioning to a set of French doors at the opposite end of the lobby. "But room service is open all night. Just dial seven on your room phone."

Josh's eyes widened. "Perfect!"

"How can you possibly be hungry?" said Mr. Cawston. "You ate two dinners."

"Not to mention all the chips and chocolate bars in the car," added Kara.

"That was light-years ago," he scoffed.

Quinn searched the lobby for a clock but couldn't locate one. "What time is it anyway?"

Mrs. Cawston pulled out her phone and tried to power it up. She pressed the button twice, but nothing happened.

"Dead," she sighed, plunking it into her purse. She unzipped the overnight bag and rifled through it. "Oh no. I must have left the wall charger in the car."

"I'll get it when I park," said Mr. Cawston.

"The valet has already parked your car," said Persephone. "And unfortunately there's not much use in charging your phone. Service tends to fade in and out around here. Mostly out."

Kara's dad searched his pockets. "I guess I left the keys . . ."

"But . . . my *tablet*," whined Josh.

Kara's mother cast him a frustrated look. Then she placed a hand on Mr. Cawston's shoulder. "You're exhausted, honey. Don't worry about the charger. Let's get some rest." She eyed Josh and frowned. "A quick snack and then bedtime." She picked up the overnight bag and took one of the keys.

"First floor. Follow the hall to your left," said Persephone. "We hope your stay is a pleasant one. Don't hesitate to let us know if there's anything else we can do. We want your stay to be relaxing and enjoyable."

"I'm sure it will be," said Mrs. Cawston.

While everyone headed across the lobby, Quinn lingered a moment by the counter.

Persephone picked up the fountain pen, dipped it into the inkpot, and was about to write further in the book when she realized Quinn was peering over the counter. She shut the book and smiled. Quinn offered a weak grin and then left the counter. Phony.

As she walked, Quinn examined the elaborate woodwork. All the archways and walls were trimmed with carvings—faces of people and creatures with strange expressions.

Outside, the desert was dark, transforming all the windows into large mirrors that reflected the inside of the hotel. It reminded Quinn of a carnival fun house, where you couldn't tell what was real from reflection.

Midway across the lobby, a hand reached out and grabbed her wrist. Quinn gasped and swung around.

It was the old man. She hadn't realized she'd been walking so close to him. He lowered his newspaper, revealing sunken eyes and skin so thin it was practically transparent. Veins and vessels wove lacy patterns across his cheeks and hands. He drew her in close.

"They're going to do it."

Quinn tried to break free, but the man was surprisingly strong. She had to practically pry his fingers from her wrist.

"They're going to pull the plug," he whispered.

Quinn's pulse beat quicker. Strangers frightened her. She nodded and backed away.

Turning quickly, she nearly ran right into Persephone. The lobby was nearly empty. Quinn searched for Kara, but she had disappeared into the hallway. Quinn's chest tightened. She swallowed hard. She shouldn't have lagged behind. She shouldn't have left Kara's side.

Persephone bent toward the old man and spoke softly. "They're all here, Mr. Mirabelli."

The old man's eyes were wide and glassy. "Everyone? Even Jeanette?"

Persephone nodded. "Flew in this evening." She spun him around and wheeled him toward the elevator. No sooner had she hit the button than the cramped metal cage descended.

The door opened and the orange-haired elevator operator appeared. Her smile was big and bright just like the doorman's. Just like Persephone's. As though all the employees at Inn Between took some kind of smile training.

"Boarding pass?" she asked.

Mr. Mirabelli looked confused.

"Now, now, Sharon," said Persephone. "Stop teasing." She turned toward Quinn. "Sharon likes to pretend the elevator is an airplane."

Quinn looked at Sharon and smiled awkwardly. It was odd, though Quinn supposed it must be pretty boring to ride an elevator all day long. Airplanes were definitely more exciting.

Persephone pushed Mr. Mirabelli into the cage and closed the gate. He watched Quinn, his eyes glassy and yellowing, as the elevator thrummed its way upward.

As soon as the elevator disappeared, the lobby door burst open and a tall, unshaven man staggered inside. He wore a black ball cap with a yellow rim and a penguin logo on it. The wavy black hair that poked out beneath the cap was matted. He seemed breathless and distraught, searching the space as though not quite sure where he was. Then his gaze settled on Quinn. He stared at her long and hard, like he somehow recognized her. His bloodshot eyes sent shivers skittering up Quinn's spine.

She took a step backward and spun on her heels, hurrying into the corridor to catch up to Kara. Behind her, Quinn could hear Persephone's chirpy voice echoing through the lobby.

"Welcome to Inn Between. We've been expecting you."

6

The bell rings.

Quinn and Kara are caught in the rushing river of bodies streaming into the halls. The air is ripe with the aroma of half-eaten lunches, woolly jackets, and sweaty sneakers. Lockers clang open and shut.

Quinn beams. Her green eyes twinkle. "Did you see that goal?"

"The ball grazed the side of my head!"

She pats Kara on the shoulder. "Great reflexes!"

"I don't know why you insist on picking me first," sighs Kara. "You could choose someone good like Tyler or Jackson."

"I've told you a thousand times," says Quinn. "You are good.

You just need to stay focused on the game. Quit cloud-watching."

"I wasn't cloud-watching," scoffs Kara. She raises her chin indignantly. "I was studying the atmosphere. I think it might snow tomorrow."

Quinn rolls her eyes, though the idea of snow excites her. The slopes might open early this year. She can't wait to hit the hills. Of course her parents have taken away her first month of skiing because of those two failed science tests.

She rips off her jacket. Her thumb zips over her lock and she opens the door. Her locker is pickled with junk. A math textbook, a crumpled piece of paper, and a banana fall out. She picks them up and shoves them back inside, using her jacket to keep more stuff from escaping. "What do we have this afternoon?"

Kara hangs her jacket on a hook. She checks herself in the pink-magnet-framed mirror on the inside of her locker door. She smooths her already impossibly smooth hair, then consults the timetable she's attached below the mirror with three tulip-shaped magnets.

"Science. And then Spanish." Her books are stacked in a neat pile on the top shelf. She withdraws two textbooks and her binder. "Our assignment's due."

The air catches in Quinn's throat. She stares at Kara, her eyes saucer-wide.

"You did your Spanish assignment, right?" says Kara.

Quinn gulps. "I-I meant to . . . but . . ."

Kara's shoulders drop. She tilts her head and exhales.

Quinn can feel the heat rising into her cheeks. Her mind races like a mouse in a maze. She yanks her binder out of her locker and rips out a blank piece of paper. "Quick!" she says. "Gimme yours."

"What?" Kara takes a step back. "No way."

"Come on," pleads Quinn. "There's no time. Give me your paper. I'll change a few words. Señora Márquez will never know."

Kara shakes her head. "Nuh-uh. I reminded you every day last week. I even told you I'd help. I'm not giving you my assignment. That's not fair."

Quinn can already picture Señora Márquez as she tells the teacher her assignment is not done. The woman's face will sag with that drippy look of disappointment. She'll shake her head slowly. Then walk away. Like Quinn is a lost cause.

Then Quinn sees her parents. Her mother, the dentist. Her father, the lawyer. They are not disappointed—they are angry. They don't understand. Quinn must be brilliant. Just like they are. Just like Emma is. It's genetic, right? The teachers have it all wrong. Quinn's parents insist there is no learning disability. Quinn is just lazy. That's all. She's not trying hard enough. She should work harder. They've already taken away a whole month of skiing. Now they'll take away the entire season. Quinn will have to spend Sundays with Aunt Deirdre and her stinky pet chinchillas, while the rest of the family hits the slopes.

A watery skin covers Quinn's eyes. "Please," she whispers.

Kara's lips are sewn tight. She is frowning hard. Quinn can tell she doesn't want to bail her out—not this time. But as they stare at each other Kara softens. She opens her binder and takes out her assignment.

The crowd is thinning. Most of the kids are in class. There's no time to copy here. Quinn will take the paper to science class. She sits near the back anyway. No one will notice her copying. It will be okay.

Emma is skipping to her third-grade class. She stops in front of Quinn. "What are you guys doing?" she asks cheerfully.

Quinn snatches the paper from Kara. "Nothing."

Kara glares at Quinn, then turns toward Emma. "Hey, Em." She shuts her locker and heads toward science class.

Quinn tucks the assignment into her binder and hurries after Kara. She glances over her shoulder. She's left Emma standing alone in the hallway.

7

The hallway stretched on and on. It turned a corner, went up a short flight of steps, turned another corner, and continued.

Paintings lined the walls. Portraits and landscapes in dark, crackly oils. Most details were lost in the dim light of the cast-iron sconces topped with bronze candles and bulbs shaped like flames. Quinn hurried to catch up to Kara, who waited for her.

"Where were you?" said Kara.

"The old man stopped me—the one reading the paper."

"The guy in pajamas? What did he want?"

"I dunno," said Quinn. "I think he's a bit nutty." She

paused and then added, "And then there was this other guy—"

"This place is really beautiful," interrupted Kara. "Like a big old mansion in the middle of the desert."

Quinn glanced down the empty hallway. "Yeah. I guess. I hope the rooms aren't old and moldy."

"Let's find out," said Kara. She grabbed Quinn's wrist and pulled. When Quinn winced, she let go. "Sorry. I forgot."

Quinn blew across the wound. It was red and raw, but it was beginning to scab. "It's fine. Tomorrow it'll be good as new."

Their room was perfect. Larger and lovelier than Quinn could have imagined. Two beds with crisp white sheets and puffy rose-colored quilts stood off to the side. The antique headboards were fancier than ones she'd seen in other hotels. So were the dressers and the desk. Thick velvet drapes hung heavy and straight, framing a large window. On one wall was a tapestry with a forest scene embroidered on it. A unicorn sat peacefully in a clearing in the woods. She used to love unicorns when she was little. She secretly still loved them—though she wouldn't dare tell anyone other than Kara.

Quinn turned on the old TV that was perched on one of the dressers. It exploded into a mass of black dots that fizzed and fought their way around a blue-white screen, like a great bug-battle. Quinn decided the TV was as old as the rest of the building. An antique that belonged in the secondhand store where Mrs. Cawston loved to shop.

"No TV?" Kara plunged backward into the feathery softness of the duvet. "I'm going to miss *Math Wars*."

Quinn rolled her eyes and then flopped down beside Kara.

"You watch too much TV as is," said her mother. "Besides, we have to go to sleep. We'll be leaving early in the morning—which reminds me . . ."

Mrs. Cawston walked to the desk. The vintage phone resembled the one Quinn had seen in the lobby on Persephone's counter. She picked up the receiver and dialed zero. "An outside line, please."

She said something that didn't sound too encouraging, and then requested a wake-up call. She hung up and looked at Quinn and Kara with a curious expression.

"No outside lines," she said. "The phones are for internal use only. No wonder they didn't need a credit card. Not like we can run up long-distance charges to Mogadishu."

Quinn chuckled. Then she thought of her parents. "Mom and Dad will be worried."

Mrs. Cawston patted Quinn's shoulder. "Remember,

they're not expecting a call tonight. I'll charge my phone in the morning. We'll call them once we're on the road—just as soon as I get a signal." She smiled reassuringly.

Quinn nodded. Mrs. Cawston had warned her parents the drive might take two days. Plus, her parents were supposed to be spending the time alone together. The therapist had said it was a good idea. For them. And for Quinn. It was the only reason they'd agreed to let Quinn go. They weren't supposed to worry about her. And she wasn't supposed to worry about them. That was the deal. Quinn sighed. She wasn't holding up her end of the bargain.

"I love this place," said Josh, bursting through the adjoining doors between the hotel rooms. He threw himself face-first onto the bed beside Quinn and Kara. He flipped over, stared at the unicorn tapestry, and frowned. "Our room's way cooler."

Kara and Quinn walked through the open doors that now formed an archway between the two rooms. Josh was right—his room was very different. It had two queen beds as well, but the decor was modern, like the room had recently been renovated. The wallpaper had stars, moons, and planets. And there were two huge framed pictures of distant galaxies that looked like they were taken by the Hubble Space Telescope.

Quinn sat down on the edge of a bed. The quilt was navy corduroy—soft but not silky.

"Time for room service," said Josh, swaggering in through the adjoining doors.

"All you think about is food," said Kara.

"Pretty much." He grinned.

Kara rolled her eyes. Quinn shook her head.

Josh dialed seven just as Persephone had instructed. He ordered a large pepperoni pizza—which happened to be available. Kara and Quinn asked if they had any sort of pie. Josh checked and said they had apple, blueberry, custard, and Key lime. Kara ordered apple. Quinn chose Key lime.

Room service came almost immediately—another employee in a similar uniform. Quinn wondered how they had had time to prepare the pizza. It was like it had been ready before they even ordered.

Josh didn't waste any time wondering. He ate like a half-starved hyena. Mr. and Mrs. Cawston each had a slice, claiming it was the best pizza they'd ever had. Quinn's pie was delicious. The graham crust was sweet, with a hint of coconut, and the lime was tart—exactly the way she liked it.

"Too bad we don't have bathing suits," said Kara. "The sign said there's a pool."

"And a sauna," said Josh.

"It's late," said Mr. Cawston. "If we want to get an early start we should hit the hay." Instinctively Quinn searched the room for a clock, but there wasn't one.

"You know, Spence," said Mrs. Cawston, resting her hand on his arm and glancing around the room, "this place is so lovely. It reminds me of the vacations we used to do, before the kids."

Kara looked at Quinn and winced.

"Like that time after college when we drove along the coast in that beat-up Gremlin," she continued. "We stayed in all those little places, like the Happy Landing Inn in Carmel, and that musty old Mariners Inn in Cambria."

Mr. Cawston had the same faraway look in his eyes. "Remember how we heard that huge thunk and then realized we'd lost the transmission? We couldn't stop driving or we'd never get the car started again." He laughed.

"Yes. Well, I was thinking . . ."

"You want to stay awhile?" he said. "Hang out for a day or two and then drive on?"

"Why not?" said Mrs. Cawston. "We're in no rush. You don't start work for another week. Once we get settled and you start in at the new office we won't be able to get away. Life's about the journey, remember?"

"Can we, Dad?" asked Kara. "Please?"

"Yeah," said Josh. "This place is awesome."

Everyone looked at Quinn.

"Well," said Mrs. Cawston. "What do you think?"

Quinn smiled. "Sure. So long as we let Mom and Dad know." Kara swung her arm around Quinn and they bounced backward onto the bed.

"Of course," said Mrs. Cawston. "We'll call them in the morning. I'll charge my phone and we'll make sure we get a signal." Then she turned toward Mr. Cawston. "We'll stay a night. Maybe two. We can go for hikes in the desert, get a close look at those Joshua trees—they're blooming, you know."

"I'd love to see a blooming Josh!" Kara laughed.

"Very funny. Hey, maybe we'll see some snakes and lizards!" said Josh.

"Or aliens," said Kara.

Quinn smiled. Snakes and aliens. Perfect.

"I'll check with the front desk," said Mr. Cawston. "Make sure the rooms are available." He slipped into the hallway.

"Okay, guys. It's been a long day," said Mrs. Cawston, clapping her hands. "Time for bed. Let's go, girls."

Surprisingly, Josh didn't put up much of a fight. He was already heading toward the bathroom when the three left the room.

Kara and Quinn weren't tired. They protested, but since Kara's mother would be sleeping in the bed beside them, they didn't have much choice but to do as she said and get washed up and ready for bed.

Quinn got into her flannel shorts and favorite baseball jersey. She slipped beneath the quilt just as Kara's mom said, "Lights out."

For a while she and Kara talked in the secret language Kara had developed for use during dark sleepovers. If Quinn traced a heart on Kara's shoulder it meant *Who do you like?* Kara would spell the boy's name with her finger on the palm of Quinn's hand. If Kara touched Quinn's hand to her foot and pretended to squash it, it meant *What's bugging you?* Quinn would spell out her answer on Kara's hand.

That night Kara touched Quinn's hand to her head. This meant *What are you thinking?*

Quinn put her finger to Kara's palm and wrote one letter—E.

Kara squeezed Quinn's hand. She held it until she fell asleep.

Quinn twisted and turned beneath the covers for the longest time. Finally, she drifted off. She had no idea how long she'd been asleep when something dragged her from her dreams.

She opened her eyes but there was little difference—the room was spider-black. She never used to be afraid of the dark, but now she slept with the hall light on and her bedroom door wide open. Occasionally her mother would forget and turn out the light while Quinn was asleep. If she awoke in darkness, beads of cold sweat would skitter over her body. She'd lie frozen, unable to move, unable to breathe, until gray morning light pressed its way in through the blinds.

Here, with Kara beside her, the darkness was bearable. Quinn searched for the time but then remembered there was no clock in the room. A hollow shuddering blew past the window. She sat up and listened. It came back again and again.

Quinn slunk out of bed and walked to the window. She pulled back the heavy drapes. Darkness stretched like a gloved hand over the landscape. Only the tiniest sliver of moon lit a jagged horizon that seemed a million miles away. She breathed deeply. Bluebells. She could swear she smelled bluebells. She twisted a lock of hair between her fingers.

As Quinn rested her cheek on the cool glass, the wind swooped in and pressed against the pane. Beyond the whoosh and hiss, she heard something else. Not a hum this time, but a low, distant wail.

Quinn listened sharply. There was something familiar about the pitch—the alternating sobs and silence. Was it possible? Could it be? Questions circled themselves, knotting inside Quinn's mind. She listened again, but then suddenly the crying stopped.

Quinn took a deep breath. She was doing it again. She was imagining things. It was just a coyote. Or a bobcat.

Quinn shut the drapes and slipped back beneath the covers. She closed her eyes and lay there for the longest time until her thoughts began to melt and drift away.

The next morning, she awoke to the shrill buzzing of the telephone. It rang three times and then stopped. Their wake-up call. Mrs. Cawston had forgotten to cancel it.

The room swam in soupy darkness. Quinn sat up and switched on the bedside lamp. She yawned and stretched. Kara was still sound asleep.

The bed beside them was empty. Kara's mother was gone. The covers lay flopped over the pillow in a tangled mess. Quinn nearly looked away, but then a tiny dark speck caught her attention. It was the size of a pinhead, but it seemed to be growing.

She swung her legs around the side of the bed and stood. She was sore and wobbly, like she was using her legs for the first time in decades.

She moved toward the opposite bed. The spot on the duvet had already grown to the size of a quarter and it was getting larger and darker by the second.

Slowly, carefully, Quinn reached out a trembling hand. She grasped the corner of the pink duvet and peeled back the covers. She gasped.

On the pillow, where Kara's mother had been lying, was a pool of blood.

8

QUINN SPRANG BACK. Her heart pulsed in her throat. Blood drummed in her ears. She dove for Kara.

Kara made a soft sound, like a cooing dove. She rolled over and continued to doze. Quinn shook her hard. "Wake up, Kara. Wake up!"

Kara raised her head. She looked at Quinn through puckered eyes and yawned like she'd been asleep for centuries. "Huh? Whaa?"

"There!" Quinn yelled. "Look!"

Kara sat up drowsily. She looked around. "Where? What?"

Quinn pointed a frantic finger at the other bed, but when she turned to look at it, the blood was gone.

She leaped toward the bed and pulled back the covers.

She flopped them this way and that, but there was no trace of blood. She swore it had been there a second ago—a deep, wet stain. She picked up the pillow—it was silky white, the duvet rosy pink. She let them fall from her hands. She blinked hard and rubbed her eyes. Her mind was hazy. She must have been dreaming.

"What's wrong with you?" said Kara.

Quinn took a deep breath and exhaled. "Your mom's gone."

Kara frowned. She stretched her arms and rubbed her eyes. She looked over at the empty bed, then at Quinn's confused expression, and shook her head. "Don't worry. She's probably in the next room."

The door between the two rooms was shut. The overnight bag Mrs. Cawston had brought was gone. So was her purse. Only Quinn's shorts, Kara's skirt, and their T-shirts were left—all folded neatly in two piles on top of the dresser. The room key was placed between them.

Quinn wandered toward the window and pulled open the drapes. The sky was still dark, but a hint of blue crept over the horizon. She wondered what time it was. Probably very early, judging by the position of the sun. "Why didn't she wake us?"

Kara stepped out of bed and stretched. "I guess she wanted to let us sleep in."

Quinn grabbed her clothes and entered the bathroom to change—just in case Josh decided to barge into the room. Her whole body felt achy. She tilted her neck side to side and rubbed her arms and thighs.

She got dressed as quickly as she could. The new blue T-shirt she'd bought for the trip was wrinkled from the car ride. She didn't like the idea of wearing the same clothes two days in a row, but she could think of worse things. Like having no toothbrush. Both Kara's and hers weren't there. Mrs. Cawston must have forgotten to leave them out. Where had she moved the overnight bag?

Quinn dragged her fingers through the tangles in her hair. That's when she noticed the skin around her wrist had healed. Not scabbed over, but mended. Good as new. Like she'd never been cut at all. She slid the bracelet higher on her wrist and rubbed the spot. The wound hadn't been nearly as bad as she'd thought.

When Quinn exited the bathroom Kara was already dressed. She was slow waking, but once she got going she fizzed with energy. She had a huge smile on her face and her brown eyes sparkled.

"Can you check if your mom's in the other room? If she's there, ask her for the toiletry bag. I wanna brush my teeth."

"Okeydokey, artichokie," said Kara. She moved toward

the adjoining door, threw it open, and passed into the next room. Quinn didn't follow, just in case Josh or Mr. Cawston wasn't quite ready.

Quinn thought Kara's dad was great. Like Kara, he always wore a huge smile. He loved to tell funny stories and often surprised Kara and Josh with tickets to some ball game or movie or amusement park.

Quinn's parents used to be like that, too—happy, smiling, full of energy and fun. Now their voices were somber, their movements slow. Their words were guarded, like they could never really say what they meant. They were ghosts pretending to be people. They looked real and sounded real, but Quinn was sure if she reached out to touch them, her hand would slice through thin air.

Kara emerged from the archway. "Josh is still asleep, but my parents are gone."

Quinn gasped. "What do you mean gone?"

"As in *not there*, silly."

Quinn stared at her for a moment, calculating explanations. "Do you think they went to get breakfast?"

"Maybe," said Kara. "Or maybe they're getting some stuff from the car."

"Yeah. I'm sure that's it." Quinn smiled. "They probably went to get the charger. Your mom said she'd charge the phone in the morning."

Kara moved back toward the archway. "I'm gonna wake Josh."

Quinn returned to the window. Sunlight spilled over the landscape. The sand glistened like crushed gold. She could hear Josh grumbling in the next room.

She crossed the room and stepped into her boots. She opened the door and peeked out. The corridor was as dim as it had been the previous evening. Light sizzled from the fake candles. She searched right and left for Kara's parents.

At the far end was a trolley filled with towels, rolls of toilet paper, and tiny bottles. A short, stout maid in a black dress with a frilly white apron stood beside it. She looked up and her lips curled into a smile—the same sticky-sweet smile as on all the other employees of Inn Between. She bent her head and went about her business, dumping a wastebasket into a trash bag attached to the trolley's end.

Quinn shut the door. She didn't want to run into anyone, especially the old man from the night before.

Josh stumbled into the room, his shirt hanging out of his jeans, and flopped onto the bed where his mother had slept. "Where are they? I'm starved."

Kara rolled her eyes. "You're so predictable."

"And you're so annoying." He threw a pillow at her.

Quinn caught it. "Stop bickering, children," she said,

imitating Mrs. Cawston. "Or I'll call the mother ship to beam you both up."

Kara and Josh laughed.

Josh tried the TV. Channel after channel was filled with nothing but black and white dots. They watched the frenzy for some time in silence, but no one came.

"Where could they be?" asked Quinn.

Kara shrugged. "You know them. They like to wander off on their own. They're weird like that."

Quinn nodded. It was true. The Cawstons could be unpredictable. "But don't you think it's strange—even for them?"

"Maybe." Kara sighed. "But I gave up trying to figure them out ages ago."

Josh's stomach rumbled. He sprang to his feet and shut off the TV. "Let's go. They're probably having coffee. Maybe eating without us." The thought seemed to trouble him immensely.

"He's right," said Kara. "Besides, this room is starting to make me feel claustrophobic."

"Should we leave a note?" asked Quinn.

"Good idea," said Kara. She rifled through the dresser drawer and found a pad of paper and a pen. She quickly jotted down a few words and left the paper on the bed.

The three headed through the halls toward the main

lobby, Josh up front, Kara in the middle, and Quinn bringing up the rear. They made it all the way to the enormous lobby without meeting a single soul.

Morning light streamed in through the long, lean windows. In the lemony glow, the lobby was even more beautiful than Quinn remembered—the most beautiful hotel she'd ever seen.

As she stared at the gilded wallpaper and interesting artwork, a grinding noise stole her attention. The elevator was heading upward. She caught sight of the operator's legs standing beside a passenger wearing beige polyester pants with matching beige support shoes.

"I so want to ride that thing," said Josh. "It reminds me of the elevator in that horror movie. You know, the one where those three kids are trying to escape a city full of postapocalyptic zombies and they race into this old building and jump in the elevator, only the elevator is jammed and a zombie reaches in and pulls the one guy right through the bars, totally shredding him?"

"Charming," said Kara.

"I'll stick to the stairs," said Quinn.

"Suit yourself." Josh shrugged. He left the girls to wait by the elevator, apparently forgetting his stomach and his parents for the moment.

Persephone was behind the front desk, busy checking in

a new guest. Quinn decided she must work long shifts. Maybe she even lived at the hotel. Maybe all the employees did—after all, the hotel was pretty far from civilization. If anything, they'd have a very long commute.

The new guest was a young woman. Her long dark hair was damp. So were her clothes. Her eyes were glassy and listless, her face puffy, her lips marbled. She wasn't carrying any luggage.

Quinn's eyes met the woman's, and for a moment Quinn thought she seemed frightened.

Quinn and Kara exchanged glances.

The woman was about to say something, but Persephone interrupted. "Your key, Ms. Khan. Let me know if there's anything else."

She stared at the bronze key for a moment, then took it and left the front desk, glancing side to side as she left the lobby.

At the far end, Quinn noticed the French doors were open. Beyond them she heard dishes and cutlery clanking. The edge of a starched white tablecloth was visible. She took Kara's arm. "Come on."

"Josh!" called Kara. "Restaurant!"

Josh tore himself from the elevator and joined the girls. They stood in the doorway searching the tables for Mr. and Mrs. Cawston.

Most people sat alone—business travelers, thought Quinn.

Though most were very old, some were really young—not much older than Quinn and Kara. They didn't look at all like they were there on business. There was no sign of Kara's parents.

A uniformed woman bustled toward them. She had definitely passed smile-school with flying colors. "Good morning. We've been expecting you."

Kara spoke up. "We're looking for my parents. Have you seen a man and a woman? Tall man, longish hair. With a woman wearing jeans and a yellow T-shirt?"

"No one like that this morning, miss," said the woman. "May I seat you?"

"Sure!" said Josh.

"Hold on," said Kara. "We have to wait for Mom and Dad. We don't have any money."

"Breakfast is complimentary," said the bubbly woman.

Josh grinned. "See. Complimentary. Don't worry about Mom and Dad—they'll find us."

Quinn looked at Kara. She raised her eyebrows.

"He's right. They're probably out for a hike," said Kara. "Some alone time." She stretched the word *alone* and rolled her eyes. "We might as well eat."

Quinn nodded. The food smelled delicious. And knowing Josh, Mr. and Mrs. Cawston would check the restaurant first.

The woman seated them near the entrance to the lobby so they could keep an eye out. Josh raced ahead to the buffet. Quinn and Kara followed.

Waves of crisp bacon, sausages glossy with grease, fluffy yellow clouds of scrambled eggs, plate-size pancakes wafting vanilla and cinnamon into the air lined the buffet. There were fresh berries and sliced pineapple and three kinds of melon balls. There was even a carving station with a huge slab of baked ham and an enormous hunk of roast beef. A man dressed in white stood behind it holding a gleaming knife, prepared to shave off a sliver.

Josh was in heaven. He piled his plate high until it was a staggering mound of breakfast delights. By the time Quinn and Kara got to the table he was already elbow-deep in sausages, eggs, and pancakes. He chomped and smacked loudly. Quinn slipped a bite of blueberry pancake into her mouth. It practically melted on her tongue.

While she ate, she studied the sea of faces at the surrounding tables. There was an old woman with cotton-candy hair and gray crinkly eyes, a man with slicked-back hair wearing a pin-striped business suit, and a young couple leaning in close talking in hushed whispers. Different complexions, different ages, yet they all shared a strange expression—as though something wasn't quite right.

"I need my wallet," whispered the young woman.

"Don't worry," said the guy with her. "They said we don't need any money."

"I want my purse back. Have you seen my purse? Someone took my purse."

At another table Quinn saw a family—a man, a woman, and a little girl. For a second she wondered if it had been the little girl she'd heard crying the previous night. It was possible.

"It's so hot in here," said the woman. She fanned herself with her hand. "I'm dying of heat."

Pearls of sweat covered the man's forehead. His face looked flushed. He mopped himself with his napkin. "The air-conditioning must be broken," he said. "I'll speak to the front desk."

Quinn frowned. She wasn't hot at all. In fact, if anything, she felt a slight chill.

While the parents continued to complain about the heat, the little girl sat silently, clutching a cloth doll. It wore a frilly green dress and had matching green shoes. Its hair was a tangle of orange wool. The girl held out her doll and smoothed down the hair. That's when Quinn noticed one side of the doll's hair was singed and part of her green dress was smudged with soot. The girl didn't seem to notice. Or perhaps she didn't care.

Beside the family sat a teenage guy with a faux-hawk.

His arms were covered in tattoos. He was bent over a steaming cup of coffee. He looked exhausted, as though he'd been up all night.

Quinn sat contemplating the strange assortment of guests. She was about to pop a bite of greasy sausage into her mouth, when her eyes fell on *him*.

In the farthest corner, draped in shadow, was the man with the black-and-yellow ball cap. Even across the crowded room, Quinn could see his bloodshot eyes examining Kara, then Josh, before settling on her.

9

QUINN'S FORK SLIPPED from her grasp. Sausage catapulted across the table.

Josh snatched it midair and popped it into his mouth. "Thanks."

"You're disgusting!" said Kara.

Quinn broke free from the man's gaze, but she couldn't shake the feeling that he was still staring at them.

"What's wrong?" asked Kara. "You look like you've seen a ghost."

"It's nothing," said Quinn. She didn't want Kara to think she was acting paranoid. Again.

Quinn forced a weak smile. She was imagining things—just like she'd imagined the blood. Like she'd imagined

Emma crying. She told herself that the man wasn't even looking at their table. He was probably just staring off into space, deep in thought. People did that sort of thing.

Kara narrowed her eyes. "There's something you're not telling me."

Quinn found her fork and began puncturing holes in her scrambled eggs. "It's nothing. Honestly." She placed a bite of egg into her mouth. It tasted like rubber.

While she chewed, she stole a glance at the far corner. The man sat straight in his chair, an empty plate in front of him.

"Best . . . breakfast . . . ever," said Josh, his mouth so crammed with bacon he could hardly get the words out. He'd cleaned his plate and was gearing up for another round at the buffet.

"Hurry," said Kara as he dashed off. "I wanna find Mom and Dad."

Where had the Cawstons gone? Kara didn't seem too disturbed by their absence and neither did Josh, which put Quinn somewhat at ease. She tried to eat a few more bites, but all the while she volleyed glances between her plate and the far corner. The man just sat there, his icy glare prickling her skin.

Josh returned with even more food than the first time. Kara and Quinn watched with a mixture of marvel and disgust as he shoveled truckloads into his mouth. Amazing he was as thin as a rail.

"Will you hurry?" said Kara.

Syrup dripped down his chin. "Quit rushing me. It's not like we have anywhere to go."

As the two argued, out of the corner of her eye Quinn registered movement. Her face shot in the man's direction. He was standing. He took a step toward their table.

She was suddenly filled with a deep sense of dread. She sprang to her feet. "We gotta go."

Kara stood in reflex. "What? Why?"

Quinn pulled Josh to his feet. "Come on. We need to leave."

"But . . . I'm not done yet!" said Josh, digging in his heels. He reached for his last bite of bacon.

There was no time to explain. Quinn had to get out of the restaurant. To get away from that man. She'd try to explain once they were a safe distance from the stranger. "Please."

Kara looked at Quinn and sighed. She nodded and grabbed Josh's other arm. "You've had enough, big brother." Together they hauled him protesting toward the exit.

Before she left the restaurant, Quinn glanced over her shoulder. The man was heading toward them. He wasn't running, but he was tall and his strides were long. He'd catch up soon enough.

Quinn searched the lobby. It was quiet and there was no place to hide. They'd never make it to the far end and down the hallway in time.

Persephone was at the front desk. Quinn motioned with her head and they hurried toward her. Something told Quinn they'd be safe near Phony.

"What was that all about?" asked Josh.

"That man, he's after us," whispered Quinn.

"What man?" said Kara, searching the lobby.

"That man," said Quinn, pointing to the restaurant doors. She watched, expecting the guy to come charging toward her any second. The only person who came out was the cotton-candy-haired woman.

Josh and Kara exchanged glances. Quinn was about to explain when Persephone interrupted.

"Can I help you?"

"Have you seen my parents?" said Kara.

Persephone stared at her, the same stubborn smile superglued to her face. Her skin was pale, almost translucent.

"Cawstons, right?" She pulled a message pad from under the counter and read. "Ah, yes. They had to leave," she said. "Car trouble. Apparently your minivan had to be towed."

"Towed?" said Josh. "Are you serious?"

"Afraid so. They said you should hang around here. Find

something to do. They said they'd be back as soon as they could."

"Well," said Kara, "that explains it."

"Great," said Josh. "My tablet's still in the car."

All the while, Quinn kept checking the restaurant doors, but the man had not come out. She took a deep breath and exhaled slowly. He hadn't been following them after all. She'd been imagining things again.

"I wonder why they both went?" said Kara. "I mean, why wouldn't Mom stay with us?"

"When are they getting back?" Quinn asked Persephone. "Did they say?"

"More important, what are we supposed to do in the meantime?" said Josh.

As if it were possible, Persephone's smile grew wider. "How about a swim? Relax. Enjoy yourselves."

"A swim?" said Quinn, still casting nervous glances at the restaurant doors. "But we don't have bathing suits."

"No problem," said Persephone. "There's a shop on the second floor. They'll have everything you need. Your parents said you could charge anything you want to the room."

"Anything? Cool!" said Josh, heading toward the elevator.

Kara frowned. "Charge anything we want?" Her parents were free spirits, not free spenders. "That's not like them."

"Don't bother with the elevator," said Persephone.

Josh swung around. "Why not?"

"It's terribly slow. There isn't much point. The stairs are far quicker."

"I want to call my parents," Kara said to Persephone. "Can I use your phone?"

"Good idea," said Quinn. "I need to call my mom as well."

The woman tilted her head. Her shoulders sagged. "I'm afraid our phones are for internal use only."

Kara deflated. "Right. I forgot."

"How about a cell?" offered Quinn. "Can we use your cell phone?"

Persephone shook her head. "Sorry. Haven't got one. Not much use around here. Like I told you last night, reception fades in and out in the desert. You almost never get any service." She perked up again. "Enjoy the pool. Just be careful. It's deeper than it appears."

Quinn looked at Kara. A silent message passed between them. They were stranded at the Inn Between.

10

Señora Márquez sits at her desk scowling.

All eyes are on Quinn. Blood has completely drained from her face. She's ghostly pale. She has never stolen anything in her life. Now she's branded a thief. A word thief. Her heart melts into a puddle beneath her desk.

Kara bites her lower lip and hangs her head. She will lose a full grade on her assignment. Señora Márquez says the cheatee is as bad as the cheater.

The teacher takes a deep breath. She says if Quinn rewrites the assignment after school, while she looks on, she will retract Quinn's failed grade. Quinn nods feebly.

Señora Márquez tells everyone to open their textbooks. Quinn tries to focus on the words in front of her, but they swim around the page. She feels the weight of stares lingering on her shoulders until the end of the day.

It's nearly four o'clock when Quinn picks up her pencil. Except for her and the teacher, the classroom is empty. The halls bare.

"You called your parents?" asks Señora Márquez. "They know you're staying late?"

Quinn can't bring her mouth to lie, so she lets her head do it. She manages a single nod.

"They're coming to pick you up?" asks the teacher. "It will be dark."

Quinn nods a second time. First a thief, now a liar. She can hear her father's disappointed voice in her head. "Oh what a tangled web we weave . . ." Quinn's web has gotten so tangled it's strangling her.

Her hand trembles as she writes. She stares at the clock, then at what she's written. She erases a chunk and begins again. She sighs. Should she use tener or haber? They both mean "to have." And here—should it be ser or estar? Why is this so complicated?

When she hands in her assignment, Señora Márquez looks it over quickly as though she's already decided on a grade. "I'm disappointed in you, Quinn," she says. "I hope you've learned a lesson."

Quinn's head bobs. Yes. Yes she has. And this time it's no lie.

It's late by the time she packs up. She has to beat Señora Márquez to the parking lot. Quinn zips through the empty halls and bursts out the front door. The sun has all but disappeared. The sky is deep purple, pressing into black. The streets seem darker than usual.

Quinn follows the same route she and Emma take every morning and every afternoon. Only it all seems strange now. Wrong.

She thinks of Emma. Though they share the same high cheekbones, the same straight nose, Quinn's cheeks are gaunt and her hair is dull. She is like a faded photocopy from a printer running out of ink. Only she came into the world first. She should be the vibrant one. Emma should be the copy. It doesn't seem fair.

The air is icy. Vapor puffs from Quinn's mouth and the wind snatches it away. Kara's right—it might snow soon. Most slopes will open early.

Quinn walks briskly. The maples and oaks lining the street are bare. Their branches stretch across the sky like cracks in a mirror. She thinks she hears footsteps behind her. The fine hairs on her neck prickle. She shouldn't be walking home alone. She breaks into a light jog, but when she glances over her shoulder, she relaxes. There's no one there.

Halfway to her house, Quinn passes the park. The swings hang silent and still. The play structure is a dark and empty shell. She doesn't notice the splash of bright orange lying on the ground next to the slide.

The front door is locked. The lights are out. Quinn rings the doorbell again and again. No one answers.

"Emma! Let me in!"

With each second that passes Quinn gets more and more frustrated. Emma's goofing around. She's trying to bug Quinn. She'll probably jump out and yell Boo! Quinn is in no mood for games.

She makes a fist and pounds as hard as she can. The old door rattles. "Emma! Come on! It's cold out here."

In the distance, headlights approach. The hum of an engine grows loud. Tires turn into the driveway, and for a moment Quinn's caught in the lights. They illuminate her briefly, then slide past and shine on the garage. They switch off.

Now Emma's done it. Mom's home. Quinn has nowhere to hide. She's caught. Her mother will find out everything and tell her father. She'll be grounded for sure. Emma should have let her in. If Quinn had made it inside even with seconds to spare, her parents would never have known she'd been late—never have known she'd been cheating on an assignment.

Quinn pounds frantically on the door, even though she knows it's too late. Her mother is already out of the car. Quinn stares at the walkway like a prisoner awaiting her executioner.

Emma is so going to pay for this. It's all her fault. Quinn will take back the purple hoodie she gave Emma—the one Emma begged her for all last year. Plus, she won't let Emma come with her and Kara to the movies on Friday—that is, if she's still allowed to go.

"What are you doing out here?" says her mother, lugging her purse and briefcase. "Why do you have your backpack? Where's Em?"

Exactly. Where is Emma?

Quinn stutters and stammers, trying to find an excuse. "I-I was . . . It's just . . . we were . . . I . . ."

The pressure is too great. The dam Quinn built to hold back her emotions bursts. Tears gush down her cheeks, and in choked sobs she tells her mother about the copied assignment. About having to stay late. "I-I'm sorry. I won't do it again."

Her mother frowns. "You're in big trouble, Quinn. And so is Emma. Why didn't she wait for you? She's not supposed to walk alone. Neither are you, especially in the dark."

Quinn drags a sleeve across her face. She has something to say. She wants to tell her mother—she should tell her—but instead Quinn's jaw clenches and her eyes narrow. She wants Emma to get in trouble. It will be payback for not opening the door. Payback for being so perfect.

Quinn's mother continues her lecture as she fishes for the key and opens the door. "How could you? I've always taught you to be honest. Why didn't you just ask for more time?"

The house is dark. Quinn's mother switches on the light and calls for Emma but there's no answer. She tells Quinn to go upstairs and look for her sister—maybe she's in the bathroom. Maybe she's listening to music with her headphones and can't hear.

Quinn lets her backpack drop. She kicks off her shoes and marches up the stairs. She wants to find Emma first—to tell her off. She is happy Emma's going to get in trouble. She wants to be the one to tell her.

Quinn doesn't find Emma. Not in the room they share. Not in the bathroom. She checks the basement. And the yard. Emma's coat is missing. So is her backpack. Emma never made it home.

11

THE STAIRCASE LED TO A NARROW BALCONY overlooking the lower lobby. To the right, a set of French doors opened onto a terrace. A plaque above the doors read *Pool*. In the opposite corner was the gift shop. Quinn stepped inside.

The space was tight and dark, more like an oversize closet. She was sure it had been nothing more than a storage room at some point.

An odd collection of junk cluttered tall shelves. Aside from the usual things you might expect to find—gum, chocolate, Band-Aids, T-shirts, earplugs, batteries—there were also candles, ceramic toads, dragons and three-headed dogs, swords, arrows, chunks of crystal, paper butterflies, dream catchers, and bathing suits.

"I am not wearing this," said Josh, holding out baby-blue shorts with white fluffy clouds and pink sheep.

"You don't have much choice," said Kara, dangling a white tankini with red polka dots. "At least you won't look like you have the measles."

The only thing in Quinn's size was a neon-green one-piece with a frilly skirt attached—the kind grandmas with varicose veins and saggy skin wore. She was surprised it didn't come with a matching bathing cap covered in rubber tulips. "I think I'd rather have the measles," she sighed.

An elderly man sat behind a small counter. Kara handed him the room key. He made note of the number and the items on a pad of yellowing paper.

"Where should we change?" Quinn asked Kara.

The man pointed a bony finger. "Change rooms by the pool. Towels are complimentary. Refreshments, too."

"I love complimentary!" said Josh.

Kara frowned. "Maybe we should go to the room. Maybe Mom and Dad are back."

"We were just at the front desk. Phony would have told us," said Quinn.

Kara looked puzzled. "Phony?"

"The clerk—Persephone. She's so fake."

Kara leaned in close as though sharing a secret. "They're all a bit weird around here."

Quinn grinned. "You noticed?"

They left the tiny shop and followed the balustrade toward the open doors. The terrace was blindingly bright—a huge contrast to the dimly lit hotel. Quinn had to shield her eyes until they adjusted. The searing heat hit her at the same time and she realized just how comfortable it had been in the cool hotel.

The pool was an enormous rectangle in the middle of a cobblestone courtyard filled with chairs and chaise lounges. A few were occupied. Most were empty.

For the first time Quinn got a better sense of the structure of the hotel. It rose up on all sides surrounding the pool. There were more floors than she'd thought. Five. Maybe seven. Every time she tried she'd lose count, and it was tough looking up into the bright sunlight. Though she'd seen the front of the hotel that one time—and it was late and dark and they had all been exhausted—its size still shocked her.

To the right was the women's cabana. Quinn grabbed two fluffy white towels from a trolley as she entered.

She slipped into the neon-green one-piece and grimaced. She'd have died a thousand deaths if she were caught in one of these back home. She told herself it didn't matter who saw her here. She'd never see any of these people again.

Kara looked slightly better in her measly suit. They pointed at each other and laughed. Quinn stopped short when she saw the bruises.

"What happened?" she asked, pointing to Kara's arms and legs.

Kara seemed as amazed as Quinn to see the purple blotches. She touched a spot on her upper arm and winced. "I don't know. I guess I bumped into something."

"You should be more careful," said Quinn. Kara smiled and nodded.

Earlier that morning Quinn had felt stiff and sore. As she slathered on sunscreen, she moved her arms, her neck—the soreness was fading. Hopefully Kara's bruises would heal as quickly.

When both were ready, they stepped outside. Josh had organized a group of chaise lounges under a large umbrella. "Ha!" he said when they got near. "You guys look hilarious."

"Baa, baa, black sheep," sang Kara, tossing her towel onto a chair.

Josh's grin fell. "Very funny," he grumbled. Then he perked up. "Hey, listen—we can have lunch here. They've got hot dogs and fries." He pointed to a kiosk at the far end of the pool.

Quinn rolled her eyes and sank into a chaise. "I swear, there's something wrong with you."

Josh left his towel and clothes on his own chaise and headed for the water. Kara followed. They hobbled over hot cobblestones. Josh jumped into the water first, making a huge splash. Kara slipped in after him.

"Hot, eh?" said a gravelly voice.

Startled, Quinn looked up to see the guy with the faux-hawk hovering over her. She took a deep breath, relieved it wasn't the man with the ball cap.

He sat down in the empty chaise beside her. He wore a light blue bathing suit with yellow umbrellas. He must have gotten it from the gift shop. It seemed out of place on a body with so many tattoos. He held a tall glass of water with a lemon wedge stuck on the rim. "Nice place. Relaxing."

Quinn smiled and nodded.

"They could use some cooler bathing suits, though." He chuckled.

"Yeah." Quinn laughed nervously, smoothing down her neon-green skirt.

He took a long-drawn sip through a pink straw. "Name's Rico. What's yours?"

"Quinn."

He took his lemon slice, squeezed it, and plopped it into his glass. "So, Quinn. Who sent you?"

She wrinkled her brow. "Sent me?"

"To this hotel. For rest. That's why you came, isn't it?"

"Nobody sent us," she said. "We just stopped here. On our way."

Rico glanced around at the building and the pool. "Funny thing. I was at this party. I guess things got out of hand. Next thing I knew, I was here and they were telling me to relax. Enjoy myself."

Quinn kept silent as Rico told her about how he'd been in trouble a few times, but that this time his parents had probably had enough and sent him to this place to get straightened out.

"Quinn!" called Kara. "Come on!"

Quinn scrambled to her feet, relieved to get away from the awkward conversation.

Rico got up as well. "See you around."

She fanned her fingers. "Sure."

Quinn took a few steps and the soles of her feet were on fire. She raised her toes and walked on her heels all the way to the pool. Lowering herself onto the cement edge, she dipped her feet into the cool water.

The pool shimmered like a great blue jewel. The water was clean and fresh. No sharp smell of chlorine bit her nostrils like it did at other public pools. Perhaps it was salt water.

"Who was that?" asked Kara.

"Some guy," said Quinn, glancing over her shoulder. Rico was halfway to the hotel doors.

Sunlight danced on the tips of waves as they lapped and swashed gently against her shins. She gripped the pool's edge with both hands, pushed off, sinking beneath the glassy surface.

The world around her disappeared. Silence closed in on her as she sank deeper and deeper. For a moment Quinn forgot where she was. For a moment everything washed away—her fear, her worry, the constant pain of not knowing. And for a moment—just a moment—she thought she heard Emma's voice.

Quinn opened her eyes.

Light rippled downward from the surface, casting distorted shadows into the depths. Kara's body was high above. Quinn could see her legs gently paddling. Below, the water was dark. Bottomless.

Quinn's gaze ran the length of the pool. At the far end, a shadow rose. It seemed to have a human form, but it cut through the water sleek and fast like nothing human could.

Panic pressed the oxygen from Quinn's lungs. Bubbles

exploded from her nostrils. The shadow torpedoed toward her. Whatever it was, it was after her.

Quinn thrust her body upward. She made it halfway to the surface when an icy hand grabbed her left ankle. She kicked and flailed but the grip only tightened.

Quinn's chest throbbed. She needed air. Soon she'd have to take a breath. If she didn't make it to the surface, she'd be sucking in water. She twisted and writhed, desperate to free herself, searching frantically for Kara, but everything was lost in the rippling shadows of the water that now seemed murky and green. Whatever had her leg began dragging her down.

Quinn flapped her arms harder. Her lungs were screaming for air. She'd have to open her mouth. She couldn't wait any longer. Then with a final burst of strength she kicked wildly and furiously with her right foot. Her heel struck something hard and she was suddenly free.

She propelled upward, her arms and legs pumping and pushing against the water as heavy as cement. Her body ached under the strain, but she managed to break through the surface, sputtering and gasping for air. She didn't stop until she found the pool's edge.

Placing her palms flat on the stone, Quinn hoisted herself out of the water and onto her knees. She sat sucking in great gulps of air, searching over her shoulder for the shadowy figure. All she saw was clear blue water and lacy patterns of flickering light.

Kara swam toward the edge. "What's up?"

"You're not going to make us leave the pool like you did the restaurant, are you?" Josh sighed.

Quinn searched the water. She couldn't understand it. She'd seen that shadow. She'd felt its icy grip. It had tried to drown her. She desperately wanted to tell Kara what she'd seen—what she'd felt—but what could she say? The glassy blue water was calm and serene. There was no shadowy figure lurking there now. Kara and Josh were the only people in it. Quinn wasn't sure she'd believe her own story.

"What's wrong?" asked Kara.

"I-I don't know," she stammered. "I just needed air. I must have gone too deep."

Kara glanced at Josh. She put her hands on the pool's edge and then slung her arms over it. "But," she said softly, gingerly, as if Quinn were a glass figurine, easily broken, "the pool's only six feet deep."

Quinn studied the shimmering surface again. Along the sides were painted markers she hadn't noticed before. Four feet in the far end. Six feet below.

"But . . . the bottom . . ." she began. Her voice trailed off as Josh dipped, touching the base of the pool with flat feet. He held his arms straight up. The water barely covered the tips of his fingers. Quinn rubbed her temples. She hadn't imagined the depth. She couldn't have. Could she?

Despite Kara's coaxing, Quinn refused to enter the water again. Instead, she lay on a chaise under the canopy of the umbrella as the morning melted away.

Kara insisted Josh check the front desk to see if their parents had returned. He made several trips, each time returning with no news.

Kara alternated sitting with Quinn and cooling herself in the water. She tried to get Quinn to join her, but Quinn wanted nothing to do with the pool.

Quinn closed her eyes. Even out of the direct rays of the sun, her skin burned. Each breath sent searing air into her lungs. But she resolved not to go back into the pool, not even if she burst into flames.

Judging by the sun's position it was now afternoon. Kara's parents had been gone for such a long time. They had to be back soon.

Above, black dots circled. Turkey vultures. Their movement was mesmerizing. Quinn watched for a long time. Round and round and round. She was about to search the pool for Kara when her eyes snagged on a window in the topmost floor of the hotel.

She saw a figure framed in glass. And though the sun was blindingly bright and the window way up high, Quinn was positive she recognized the silhouette—a slight figure. Wearing a pink cap . . .

Quinn slid from the chaise. The world around her swirled to black.

12

"Emma!"

Quinn stands at the edge of her driveway, yelling into the dark street. The front door is wide open. She hears her mother's frantic voice drifting out from the living room. She's on the phone, speaking to Quinn's father, who is late at the law firm as usual. Quinn catches bits and pieces, though she's only half listening.

". . . heard from Emma? Did she call you? . . . not home. No, they didn't come home together . . . worried sick."

They didn't come home together. Home together. The words rise and fall in Quinn's mind like an echo.

"Call family," says Quinn's mother. "I'll try friends. Neighbors. Come as fast as you can."

It's a new moon. The sky is black. Quinn searches up and down the street but there is no sign of her sister. Quinn wants to run one way, then the other. Instead she is paralyzed, frozen to the spot, while her mother is driven into motion.

"Quinn!" her mother yells. "Get back inside!"

But Quinn can't move. She can't leave the driveway. Fear, like black ink, has seeped inside her, pooling in her bones. The wind slashes her cheeks and hands. She barely notices.

Quinn's mother calls more people—all of Emma's friends. Emma has lots of friends. Everyone loves Emma. But no one has seen or heard from her. Not since school ended.

". . . Yes . . . Yes . . . Come. You can help. Please."

Quinn can barely breathe. Her heart has stopped pumping. The blood has stopped flowing in her veins. She has turned to wood and grown roots.

Emma is okay, she tells herself over and over. She's gone off somewhere. She's hiding. She'll show up in a few minutes smiling her brightest smile and asking what all the fuss is about.

"Quinn!" yells her mother a second time. "Come inside!" She's holding her cell phone. She reaches for Quinn as she dials 9-1-1.

"My daughter . . ." she huffs, ". . . she's missing . . ." She gives them a description. Fair. Auburn hair. Hazel eyes. Tall for her age. She gets lost in the details of Emma's beautiful face.

Everything is happening in a blur of sound and motion.

Quinn's father arrives. So do the police. Friends and family prepare to search. Everything whirs in and around Quinn as though she's not there, as though she's slipped into another dimension—one that moves at an entirely different pace, one that is deaf to the sights and sounds of this world.

Kara arrives. She takes Quinn by the hand, dragging her back to the real world. She walks Quinn inside.

The police question Quinn. She answers them mechanically. She tells them how she had to stay late at school, about the copied assignment. She says she's a thief. A word thief. She tells the story over and over so many times she loses count. She tells them everything—every last detail—but one. She can't bear to tell anyone that. Not even Kara.

The neighborhood is alight with flashlights. Police and neighbors and friends are searching. Quinn watches through the front window. She wants to be out there searching, too, she begs to go, but her parents force her to stay behind. Mrs. Cawston and Kara have to practically hold her down.

"Let me go," she says, struggling. "I should be out there. I have to find Emma. I have to be the one."

Kara talks quietly. She calms Quinn, tells her everything will be okay. Emma will be home soon. Kara is so positive, so reassuring, Quinn almost believes her.

Each second passes like a thousand eternities. Quinn sits, just breathing, trying to make sense of what's happened. What is still happening. It's like everyone and everything is slipping and sliding away from her. If only she can sit still long enough, if she can just keep breathing, she can hold it all together.

A policewoman enters the house followed by Quinn's mother. She carries something. Quinn sees it and it's like a hard punch to her stomach. She can't breathe. It's as though some invisible beast has sucked up all oxygen, leaving barely enough for Quinn to fill half her lungs. Nothing will ever be okay again. Nothing. She crumples to a heap on the floor, sobbing and gasping for air.

The officer holds Emma's orange backpack.

13

COLD WATER SMACKED QUINN'S FACE. Her eyelids fluttered.

"Quinn? Quinn? You okay?"

The world fizzed into focus. Kara was inches away, her expression twisted with worry. Quinn tried to sit up, but sank back onto the hot cobblestones. "Emma," she muttered. "Em."

Kara and Josh exchanged curious glances.

"Heatstroke," said Josh. "I told her to come into the water."

"Hush," said Kara. "Give me that glass."

Quinn held up a limp hand and turned away. She thought Kara was going to douse her again with ice water. Instead, Kara slipped her arm under Quinn's neck.

"Here. Take a sip."

Kara tipped the glass, just enough to wet her friend's lips. Quinn opened her mouth and let the cool liquid run down her throat. She took another sip and raised her head. She gripped Kara's shoulder. "It's Emma. She's here."

Kara took a deep breath and exhaled slowly. She looked at Josh, then back at Quinn. "You passed out. You must have been dreaming." Her voice was soft and comforting, but her words were firm.

Quinn searched past Kara, past Josh, toward the hotel. She squinted and scanned each of the windows of the top-most floor. There was no pink-capped figure staring down at her. She couldn't understand it. She was so sure.

"Listen, Kara. I saw her. She's here. Emma is here." Quinn hoisted herself back onto the chaise and took the glass from Kara's hand. She drank a few more mouthfuls and set it down. "You have to believe me. I saw Emma. It was her."

"Riiight," said Josh slowly. "Like the time you saw her at the zoo?"

"And the time we had to chase after that girl at the mall with the same jacket as Emma?" said Kara.

"And all those pink caps," added Josh.

She shook her head. "This was different. I swear. This time I really saw her. I have to find her." She tried to stand, but Kara pulled her down.

"Quinn. You passed out. You must have thought you saw her. Josh, go get help."

"I'm fine." Quinn shrugged free from Kara's hold.

She stood up, still a bit weak in the knees, steadying herself against the top of the chaise, and stepped into her boots. She darted toward the side of the hotel where she'd seen Emma, shading her eyes, searching all the windows once again. She could feel the other guests watching her, including Rico, but none of them mattered. All that mattered was Emma.

"Satisfied?" called Josh.

"Emma is here. I know she is." Under her breath, she added, "And I'm going to find her."

Without warning, Quinn sprinted the length of the pool toward the entrance to the hotel. Over her shoulder, she heard Kara shouting.

"Quinn! What are you doing? Josh—grab your stuff! Quinn! Wait!"

Before Kara could catch her, Quinn ducked inside the hotel, made a sharp turn, and disappeared into the corridor that led into the wing where she'd seen Emma. Behind, she heard Kara's muffled calls, but Quinn wasn't going to stop, not until she'd found her sister.

The hallway seemed endless. Quinn ran as fast as her jittery legs would carry her. She searched frantically past door after door for a stairwell that could not be found. Somewhere on the topmost floor, Emma was waiting. She had to get to her—before she disappeared again. Before it was too late.

Quinn turned several corners, stumbled up two or three steps, then hurtled down a few more. She twisted and turned through the hallway that rose and fell, coiling through the hotel like a giant snake. In the back of Quinn's mind this didn't seem architecturally right, but she pushed the thought far away. There was no time to think about anything except Emma.

At an intersection, Quinn halted briefly, catching her breath. She searched left, then right, then straight ahead, unsure which path to take. Kara's calls had long disappeared and suddenly Quinn felt very alone.

There had to be an emergency stairwell or an elevator somewhere. If only she could find it. She scrambled a few steps to the left, when she came to a complete and dead stop.

Ahead, a figure stood by a door. She recognized the yellow-and-black ball cap. Quinn's heart, already beating out of control, threatened to burst through her rib cage. She could hear blood thudding in her ears, but she willed herself to remain statue still.

The man was bent, fumbling with a key. He was cursing

violently. Quinn was not fifty feet away, but luckily he hadn't noticed her.

Slowly, carefully, she took a step backward, certain any quick movement would draw his attention. One foot, then another, her palms cold and clammy. She hesitated, her body tense, like a sprinter waiting for the blast of a gun.

The key didn't seem to be working. The man raised his head and cursed, and just as he was turning in her direction Quinn made her move. She wheeled around and, legs pumping, she bolted back the way she'd come.

Ducking around the corner, Quinn scrambled through the intersection and plowed straight into Kara, sending both of them flying, landing flat on their backs. The clothes Kara had been holding scattered.

"What's wrong with you?" said Kara. "How could you take off on us like that?" But Quinn was already up, dragging Kara to her feet, scooping up their clothes and pulling her toward the upper lobby through the open space.

"Quinn. Stop," said Kara, digging in her heels.

Quinn yanked harder, pulling Kara toward the stairs. She scrambled down step after step. Once they reached the bottom, they paused long enough to scan the upper lobby.

All was quiet. There was no sign of the man with the ball cap. Quinn had been lucky. He hadn't seen her. She bent over, her hands on her thighs, catching her breath. How could she explain her fear of him? There was no rational reason—just a deep, dark feeling.

"You have to stop doing this," said Kara. "You have to stop imagining people are after you."

"But Emma," said Quinn between gulps of air.

Quinn felt a cool hand on her back. She looked up and saw Persephone.

"Are you all right? Can I help you?"

"Yes," said Quinn quickly, straightening her back, calming her breathing. "I need to get upstairs. I need to find somebody. Is there a way up?"

"The elevator," she said, pointing toward the metal cage. "Except, it's been slower than usual today."

"Is there no other way, then?" said Quinn. "This is a pretty big building for such a small elevator."

"It's an old building. We're up to code, of course. There's an emergency stairwell at the end of each corridor."

"Really?" said Quinn. "Because I couldn't find one."

"Oh, they're a bit tricky to find. Why do you need to go upstairs? Your room is on the first floor."

"Yes," said Kara. "It is. Let's go back to our room," she said to Quinn. "I told Josh to meet us by the door. He's probably waiting."

"Just a second," said Quinn. She turned to Persephone. "I need to find another guest. Can you help?"

"I can try," said Persephone.

Kara rolled her eyes but said nothing. Quinn left her standing at the base of the steps. At the front desk, Persephone had already taken out her guest book.

"Date?" she said.

"Excuse me?" said Quinn. "Don't you mean name?"

"No," said Persephone. "We go by dates here. Much easier to track. When did the guest arrive?"

Quinn sighed. "I-I don't know. Her name is Emma. I don't know when she would have arrived."

Persephone raised an eyebrow. "Hmm. Well. That's a bit more difficult, isn't it? Emma. Emma what?"

"Emma Martin."

"Martin? Isn't that your surname?"

"Um, yes," said Quinn, then redirected the conversation. "You really need to get some computers. Would be a lot easier."

"We prefer to keep things simple," Persephone said, flipping through the goose-fat pages, her long, lean finger scanning up and down the names she'd scrawled in fancy script and then crossed out.

"Why are they all crossed out?"

"To keep track of who's come. And gone," said Persephone. She met Quinn's eyes head-on. "Sorry," she added quickly. "No Emma."

Quinn leaned over and snuck a peek at the book. Before Persephone snapped it shut, she saw something very strange.

Kara approached the counter. "Come on, Quinn. Let's go back to the room. My parents are probably back. And Josh is waiting."

Quinn glared at Persephone a moment longer. Her face seemed so perfect. So plastic. Her eyes wide and unblinking. The woman placed her two hands on the cover of the book, then picked it up and stowed it neatly under the counter.

Reluctantly, Quinn drew back from the desk. She followed Kara into the corridor that led to their room. Her mind had left the crazy man with the ball cap and even Emma for the moment. All she could think about was the guest book and what she'd seen.

14

No one was waiting for them by the door.

"I told Josh to wait right here," sighed Kara. "No one ever listens to me."

"Maybe he's inside, with your parents," said Quinn, trying to sound hopeful even though an alarm rang inside her.

Kara got the key from the pocket of her shorts and unlocked the door. The room was empty. There was no sign of Mr. or Mrs. Cawston. Kara's note was still lying on the bed where she'd left it—untouched.

They quickly crossed the threshold into Josh's room. He wasn't there either. Something about the room seemed different, too. Everything was neat and tidy. There was no trace of Josh or Mr. Cawston, as though they hadn't been there. They searched, but neither Josh nor Kara's parents had left a note.

"Where do you think Josh went?" said Quinn, trying desperately to squelch the panic rising in her throat.

"It's nearly dinnertime," said Kara. "You know him. He probably went looking for food."

"Probably," said Quinn, her voice barely a whisper.

"Either that, or back to the pool. Maybe the elevator."

They returned to their room and got changed quickly. Quinn slipped into her shorts and T-shirt. Kara hung her wet bathing suit in the bathroom. Quinn's was dry, so she folded it and placed it on the dresser.

"I'm going to kill him," said Kara, stomping out into the hallway. "I can't believe he'd just leave us like that."

Quinn felt sick. This was her fault. If only she hadn't raced off to find Emma. She wanted to tell Kara what she'd seen in the book, but she didn't want to worry her. Not just yet. "I'll bet he's in the restaurant," she said, her voice thick, not far from tears.

"Yeah, well, he'd better be enjoying his meal 'cause it's his last."

When they reached the lobby, Persephone looked up from her work at the front desk and smiled.

"I'm looking for my brother. Have you seen him?"

Persephone tilted her head. She paused to think. "No. Not since this morning when you went to the upper lobby."

"What about my parents?" said Kara. "Have they tried to call? Left a message? You can get outside calls, can't you?"

Persephone smiled. "Of course we can. But I'm afraid I haven't heard from them. Not yet. The garage must be busier than usual. Or maybe your car needed special parts."

"You're sure Josh wasn't hanging around the elevator?"

"Not that I saw," she said. "Though, I must admit, I wasn't paying close attention. Quite a few new guests arrived today. I'll keep an eye out for him, if you like."

Just as Quinn had suspected—Phony would be no help whatsoever. Quinn grabbed Kara's arm. "Let's check outside."

They crossed the foyer and swung open the enormous wooden door. The massive doorman stood blocking their exit.

"Can I help you two ladies?" he said in his deep, velvety voice. Quinn noticed his brass name tag: Aides. His black pupils were enormous. They reminded Quinn of insect eyes.

"Have you by any chance seen my parents? Or my brother?" asked Kara. Though she was trying to sound calm, Quinn could hear worry creeping into Kara's voice.

Quinn searched beyond the red canopy, beyond the driveway. Enormous hills of gravel and dust surrounded the hotel like the sandy walls of a fortress. The small dirt road that had led them to the hotel wound through the hills, disappearing into the dust. With no map, compass, or working phone, a person could easily get lost out there.

Aides glanced thoughtfully from Kara's face to Quinn's. "Ah, yes," he said. "You came late last night. Car trouble . . ."

"The car was fine last night," said Kara. "It apparently broke down this morning. Did you see my parents? Are they back?"

Aides wiped a bead of sweat from under his cap. "Nearest garage is miles away. Only one mechanic. My best guess: they won't be back for a while." He smiled his creepy Inn Between smile.

"How about my brother? Have you seen him?"

"Sorry," said Aides, shaking his head. "Can't help you there." He placed a hand on Kara's shoulder as if to stop her from leaving. "You best stay inside. It's hotter than a skillet full of scorpions out here."

Aides was right about that. It was like a furnace out there. Quinn glanced again at the gravel road. Even if a person wanted to run away, even if they tried, they'd die quickly of exposure or dehydration if they got lost.

Aides shut the door, leaving Quinn and Kara trapped in the coolness of the lobby. Quinn turned just as the family she had seen at breakfast walked by.

"It's so hot," said the mother, fanning herself. "I'm burning up."

She took her daughter by the hand. The little girl held her rag doll. She glanced at Quinn for a moment, and Quinn saw something in the girl's dark brown eyes—a strange reflection like a flickering of yellow and orange. Then the girl turned, skipping alongside her mother and father, up the stairs toward the pool.

"I'm going to check the restaurant," said Kara.

Suddenly, Quinn had an idea. "You check the restaurant. I'll keep an eye on the elevator."

Kara nodded, then headed toward the French doors.

The fancy bars of the elevator were shut and there was no grinding noise. Quinn hit the button and waited, but nothing happened. She searched beyond the metal, craning her neck to see up the dark shaft that tunneled through the walls of the hotel like a prehistoric worm. She could see why Josh was so fascinated. Quinn shifted side to side, hoping the elevator would arrive quickly so she could check out the upper floors, but nothing stirred. Not a sign of Sharon, the elevator-pilot.

"He wasn't there," said Kara, approaching from behind.

"No sign of him here either," sighed Quinn. She covered the button with her back. She didn't want Kara to know she had planned on ditching her a second time. "Do you think he went back to the pool?"

They raced up the stairs and searched the upper lobby, the gift shop, and the pool deck. It was still hotter than Hades outside, but the sun was setting, which made the heat bearable. They searched the cabanas and called for Josh in the washroom, but there was no sign of him. Even the kiosk employee said he hadn't seen him.

"You don't suppose"—Kara paused, as though she couldn't bring herself to speak the words, then swallowed hard—"something's happened?"

"I-I dunno." Quinn's eyes flashed from the mirrored surface of the pool, up the sides of the hotel, and then back along the deck. Yes. She definitely thought something had happened. "Let's go back to the room and make a plan."

"A plan?" said Kara.

"To find everyone," was what she said to Kara. *To get out of this place,* was what she was thinking.

They arrived in front of the room and Kara took out the key. Something Persephone had said popped into Quinn's mind and she realized something about the number. "Our room number is 0708."

"So?" said Kara.

"We arrived here on the eighth of July," said Quinn, "0708."

Kara looked at the key in her hand. She looked back at the embossed brass plate on the door.

A soft cry echoed through the hall.

15

"Emma," whispered Quinn, her eyes frantic and wide.

"What?" Kara sighed. "Not again."

"Listen! Can't you hear her? She's here. She needs my help."

Quinn was about to dash in the direction of the sound when Kara grabbed hold of her arms and held tight.

"We need to focus on finding Josh and my parents. Emma's not here. Your mind is playing tricks."

"Emma *is* here. Why can't you believe me?"

Kara's eyes were fixed on Quinn. She had a strange, almost frightened look. "Emma is gone, Quinn."

The sobbing grew louder. It rippled through the hall. Then silence. Then it began again. It sounded just like Emma.

Quinn struggled to break free from Kara's grasp. "I saw her. In the window. She's here. I swear!"

"Think about what you're saying," said Kara. "It makes no sense."

"Nothing makes sense!" shouted Quinn, pulling herself free. "How can someone be there one moment and then gone the next? What sense does that make?"

Hot tears welled in Quinn's eyes. Tears of anger and frustration. She swiped at them. "Listen, Kara. Someone took Emma. What if they brought her here? What if they're holding her captive? I need to find her. Before it's too late."

"You have to stop this, Quinn. You have to stop thinking you see Emma everywhere. Hear her everywhere. Smell her everywhere."

"If it were Josh, wouldn't you want to know? What if he's the one crying? Don't you want to be sure?"

Quinn had hit a nerve. Something in Kara shifted.

"Okay," said Kara softly. "Let's make sure."

Quinn wiped her face with her arm and hugged Kara. Together they raced down the winding hallway, following all the twists and turns. They came across several intersections and each time paused to listen. Between the two of them, they figured out which direction the sound was coming from.

Finally, they ended up at the far end of a hall, in front of a room. The number was 0707. The number made no sense unless Quinn's theory was right. Whoever was in the room had arrived a day before them.

The door was shut, but beyond it the crying was clear. It was definitely a kid. Quinn pounded on the door. "Emma? Emma—is that you? Open up!"

The crying stopped. It didn't start up again.

"Are you sure this is the right room?" Kara said, staring down the long line of dark doors.

"Positive," said Quinn. She knocked again loudly. "Emma, open the door."

No response.

"Josh, is that you?" tried Kara. "Open up right now."

Silence.

Quinn took a deep breath. "Emma. Please. We'll stay here until you open the door. Or . . . or we'll call the front desk. We'll get a maid to open it for us. We'll bring the whole staff here if we have to."

Quinn heard a faint shuffling from the other side of the door, a rattle of a chain as it dropped into place, a click and a turn, and the door opened a crack, not enough to pull the chain tight. A pale blue eye stared out, looking her up and down.

Quinn's heart plummeted into her boots. It wasn't Emma. Or Josh, for that matter. Their eyes weren't blue.

The door opened a little more, revealing a round face and a thatch of blond hair, and Quinn took a step back. She knew this face. She'd seen it before. Her mind scrambled to recall.

"Wh-who are you?" said the boy. "What do you want?"

"I know you," breathed Quinn. "You're the boy—"

But before she could finish her thought, a dark shadow filled the far end of the hallway. Even in the dim light, she recognized the silhouette. It was the tall man with the ball cap.

"Let us in!" she said, her voice tight and trembling. She grabbed Kara's arm and pulled her close.

The boy startled. He was about to shut the door but Quinn stuck her hand into the gap. She yelped as he pushed against the heavy door.

"What are you doing?" asked Kara, trying to free Quinn's hand.

The man with the ball cap was walking toward them. "You!" he growled.

"Let us in!" begged Quinn. "Please."

Perhaps it was the way she said it—her voice thick and pleading—because the pressure on her arm eased and the boy stared out again.

"Please," she repeated. "We won't hurt you."

The man was halfway down the long hall. Soon he'd be on them.

"Quinn," said Kara. But Quinn pointed to the man and for the first time Kara saw him—his disheveled hair, his wild eyes glaring at them.

"You've got to let us in," said Quinn, her mind stumbling for a shred of something—anything that might help. Then it came to her. "If you help us, we'll help you find your brother."

The chain rattled and dropped. The door swung open, and the boy stepped aside. Quinn and Kara practically fell in. Quinn slammed the door behind her just as the man reached the threshold. She clicked the dead bolt and fumbled for the chain. It dropped into place and she backed up until she felt the wall at her back. Both Kara and the boy trembled beside her.

"I'm scared," he said.

Quinn put a hand on his shoulder.

"Let me in," said the man. His voice was gruff, as though crushed by years of smoking.

Quinn pulled Kara and the boy close. She huddled with them at the far end of the room, under the window, holding her breath.

A loud thump against the door made her jump. It was followed by three more thuds.

"Open up," the man grunted.

The boy searched Quinn's face as if to say, Who is that? He whimpered softly. Quinn frowned, cupped a hand to his mouth, and shook her head fiercely.

Kara gaped at Quinn. She didn't need to ask the questions; Quinn knew what she was thinking.

"Open the door," he demanded.

Kara and the boy looked at Quinn for a response, only she had none to give. She put a finger to her lips. They had to stay silent. So long as he couldn't get in, they were safe.

Quinn sank to a sitting position. The others did the same. They sat quietly, side by side, under the windowsill, listening to the man pace back and forth, demanding they open the door. All the while Quinn's mind scrambled for a way out.

Low, guttural hissing drifted in from outside. Probably vultures. Sweat prickled through Quinn's skin. She shook off the feeling. Too bad they couldn't fly out the window like a great big ugly redheaded bird.

The window. Of course. Quinn motioned for the others.

Slowly, she peeled back the curtains. Twilight splashed the sands. The sun was fading fast. Soon darkness would smother the landscape.

Quinn unlocked the hinges and carefully lifted the wooden frame. Heat rushed into the room, along with the heavy scent of creosote that smelled like rain. The hissing of the birds grew louder.

Quinn stuck her head out. Her heart sank. Though they were on the first floor, there was a dip in the grading. A thin ledge of rock, only about a foot and a half wide, ran the side of the hotel. Beyond the rocky ledge there was a steep drop.

Quinn craned her neck farther. Her gaze ran the length of the ledge along the side of the building. They weren't far from where the grading changed. If they could make it to the corner, they'd be on level ground. They could do it if they kept their backs against the wall. If they were careful. If they didn't slip. Quinn put one leg up on the windowsill.

"You're crazy," hissed Kara, grabbing her arm.

The pounding on the door was harder now, more frantic. Heavy steps paced the hallway. Breath rasping in and out. "Let me in!"

Quinn shrugged Kara off. "We have to get out of here. It's the only way." She held on to the frame and hoisted her other leg up and out the window. "I'll go first. The boy goes next. You have to help him."

Slowly, Quinn stepped onto the ledge, not putting her full weight down until she was sure it was safe to do so. With one hand still gripping under the window frame, she eased herself over, her back flat against the hot wall. From there, she made the mistake of looking down. It was at least a thirty-foot drop. And with sharp rocks and cacti below, it wouldn't be a pleasant landing. Her heart beat fast and hard. She swallowed a lump the size of a baseball.

"Come on," she said, holding a hand out for the boy, who had stuck his head out the window and was staring wide-eyed at the cliff.

"Don't look down," said Quinn. "Look at me."

She managed a weak smile, thrusting her hand farther out toward him. Slowly, he got up onto the windowsill and with Kara's help he was standing on the ledge beside Quinn, gripping her hand tightly in his sweaty palm.

They inched farther along the ledge to make room for Kara, who was already halfway out the window. She grasped the boy's trembling hand, and together they formed a human chain with Quinn leading the way.

Keeping one hand flat against the hotel wall, Quinn felt her way along the bricks. It was hot. Beads of sweat gathered under her T-shirt and trickled in a thin line down her back.

She wouldn't allow herself to look down; she kept her eyes trained on the distant horizon, on the rolling sandy hills, and on the vultures, circling and wheeling in the sky like black smoke in the wind. Adrenaline rushed through her veins, but she forced herself to take steady, calm steps, drawing the others along, inch by inch, toward safety.

They were halfway when the vultures suddenly stopped circling. One by one, they dropped, forming a single line, flying low and at great speed. They were heading straight for the ledge, squawking and hissing. Quinn thought about the vulture she'd seen by the roadside near Norm's, digging its beak into the carcass, plucking out an eyeball.

"Quicker," she yelped, gripping the boy's hand tightly, nearly pulling him off balance. He gasped and they stopped, finding their footing.

Quinn willed her feet to take steady, wide strides, as the birds drew closer, flapping their powerful wings, swooping lower, preparing to dive. The birds were less than ten feet away when Quinn's hand felt the corner of the building. She ducked around it just in time, pulling the boy with her. They fell to the ground as the birds flew past, flapping wildly, soaring off into the distance.

When the sky was clear, Quinn heaved a sigh of relief. Then she noticed Kara wasn't with them.

She sprang to her feet and dove around the side of the building. "Kara!" she yelled, not seeing her on the ledge.

"There she is!" gasped the boy, pointing a trembling finger.

Kara was sitting at the bottom of the steep incline. She had slipped off the rocky ledge, dropping about eight feet.

"You okay?" called Quinn.

Kara winced as she got to her feet. "I landed on my knee."

"Go that way," said Quinn, pointing to where the dip wasn't so steep.

Kara limped along until Quinn could reach her. She pulled Kara to level ground, slipping her arm under her shoulders.

"Those birds," said Kara. "They tried to attack us."

Quinn nodded. "They weren't the only ones."

"Who was that man?" asked Kara as they made their way back toward the front entrance of the hotel. "And why was he after us?"

"Let's get back inside, before he realizes we're not in that room anymore," said Quinn. "I promise I'll tell you everything."

Kara stopped. "I'm not moving an inch. Not until you tell me who that man was." Then she pointed at the boy. "And how do you know this guy? And his brother."

"Yeah," said the boy. "How *do* you know me?"

Quinn let go of Kara. She looked at the boy, then at her friend. "I don't know that man. I have no idea why he's after us."

"But you know something," insisted Kara.

Quinn nodded. "Last night, when we got to the hotel, you left the lobby. I stayed back."

"Because of the old man in pajamas," said Kara.

"Pajamas?" said the boy.

Quinn ignored him. "Before I left the lobby, that crazy man with the ball cap came bursting into the hotel. He stared at me like he knew me or something. It's like he's been after us ever since."

There was a long pause, as though Kara was trying to process this information. Then she added, "Okay. So he's some crazy guy who thinks he knows you. But what about this kid?" she said, pointing to the boy. "How do you know him?"

"I saw his picture in the newspaper," Quinn explained. "It said he was missing. There were two boys. Brothers."

"What newspaper?" asked Kara.

"In the diner. The one Norm—I mean Not-Norm—was reading."

The boy looked surprised. "I'm in the newspaper? Really? Are they searching for me? Who's Norm?"

"There is no Norm," said Quinn.

He looked confused.

"Why didn't you tell me any of this?" said Kara, sounding more hurt than angry. "We tell each other everything."

"I'd planned on telling you. Eventually. Once we were all safely in the minivan."

"Hey," the boy interrupted. "What about my brother? You said you'd help me find him."

"We will," said Quinn. "I promise. But first we need to get inside. Back to our room."

"She's right," said Kara. "Let's go. That man doesn't know where our room is. We'll be safe there."

"My name's Quinn," she said to the boy. "And this is Kara."

"I'm Joe," said the boy. "Glad to meet you."

16

"WELCOME BACK to Inn Between," said Aides, holding the great door open wide.

"Yeah, yeah, yeah," said Quinn. "You've been expecting us."

Joe clung to Quinn's side as they crossed the lobby. There was no sign of the man with the ball cap. Persephone was busy with another guest. They slipped into the hall, making their way back to the room.

"Here we are," said Kara, trying to sound cheerful. She dug into her pocket and pulled out the key. Thankfully she hadn't lost it. She opened the door—no one there.

Joe looked around. "Your room is different."

Quinn hadn't given it much thought when the angry

man was pounding on Joe's door, but his room had been different.

For starters, it was smaller. And there was only one bed, with a bright blue duvet dotted with footballs, soccer balls, and baseball bats. It was a kid's quilt, a kid's room—as though it had been specially prepared for him.

Quinn examined her room—the rosy quilts, the unicorn tapestry, the fluffy white pillows—these were all things she liked, things she would have decorated her room with if she'd had any say. Josh and his father's room was different altogether—more masculine, like the hotel staff knew who would be staying there.

As Quinn panned the room, her brain registered the sight at the same time as Kara. They looked at each other, and then back at the doors—the ones connecting their room and Josh's. His door was closed, and Quinn was certain when they'd last left it had been open.

Kara lunged toward the door. "Josh!" she yelled. She pounded on it with both hands but it was frozen. "Josh! Open up! Or, I swear—"

Quinn added her strength to Kara's, but the door was sealed tight, locked from the other side. "Josh? You in there?"

"Who's Josh?" asked Joe.

They stopped pounding.

"*My* brother," said Kara. "He's missing. So are my parents." Her shoulders sagged, as though it was the first time she'd admitted to herself something was wrong.

Quinn wrapped an arm around Kara's shoulders.

"But . . . you're supposed to help me," said Joe. "You said you would. The lady said someone would come to help. She said that I was in the right place—that they were—"

Quinn finished his sentence. "Expecting you?"

He nodded and sank onto the bed. Quinn let go of Kara. She sat beside Joe. He stared at her, his eyes filling with tears.

"How did you get here?" Quinn asked him.

"I came here for help. But they have no phones. No computers. They told me to stay in my room, that help would arrive soon. But I'm worried about Adam."

"Your brother?" asked Quinn.

Kara sat on the other side of Joe. "Tell us what happened and maybe we can figure something out."

"We were camping."

"Your family?" asked Kara.

Joe shook his head. "Scouts."

He explained how his troop was spending three nights in Mojave National Preserve. They were taking part in a ranger program. They did lots of things, even hiked to the base of Kelso Dunes and heard all about the mysterious singing sands.

"Singing sands?" asked Quinn.

"When the wind passes over the dunes, they sing."

Quinn thought of the humming she'd heard while they were driving—the mysterious hum that had grown louder and clearer, and then had suddenly disappeared.

"We were supposed to visit the caverns on the other side of the mountain, only all tours had been canceled because of water issues. That's when I got the idea. I told Adam we should go back to the caverns at night. We could sneak into the caves by ourselves."

Joe paused. When he spoke again it was in a low voice, barely a whisper. "We waited until it was dark, then we hiked toward the mouth of the cave and crept into the hole in the rock. We headed deeper in. Then Adam fell into some kind of pit. He was okay—but it was deep. I tried to get him to reach my hand so I could pull him up, but I slid off the edge and then we were both stuck."

Kara gasped. "What did you do? How did you get here?"

"At first we tried screaming. We screamed until our voices were hoarse. But there was no one around to hear. We were down there forever. Adam cried a lot. He was hungry and thirsty and scared. I told him everything would be okay. Someone would find us. Only no one did."

"How did you get out?" said Quinn.

"I don't know. At first, it felt like I was falling asleep. I closed my eyes—just for a moment—and when I opened them, I had this weird burst of strength. Somehow I scaled the wall. I got out and yelled down to Adam. I promised him that I would get help."

Quinn put an arm around his shoulder.

"I wandered around for a long time. Then I saw this light, in the distance. I headed for it and this is where I ended up."

Joe stared at Kara, then at Quinn, his eyes filling with tears. "It's my fault Adam is out there."

17

MONTHS HAVE PASSED. The police have called off the active search. Emma is now becoming what they call a cold case. The principal of Quinn's school suggests they hold a memorial—a vigil—that evening for Emma outside the school.

Quinn lies stretched across her bed staring at the other half of the room—the half that has not been disturbed for months. In her mind, she paints a still-life watercolor. She calls it Emma's Stuff.

*The dusty rose bedspread is bent back on itself. A wrapper from a chocolate bar Emma has eaten lies crumpled on her nightstand. Beside it lies a book—*Anne of Avonlea*. Emma loves to read. Her favorite author is currently Lucy Maud*

Montgomery, though it changes each time she starts a new book. On the shelf beside her bed are all the novels she's read. On top sits her stack of "To Be Reads."

Quinn has no such stack. She hates reading. She'd much rather ski or skateboard or ride her bike.

A purple pajama sleeve pokes out from under Emma's pillow. It dangles over the edge of the bed. Quinn thinks the pajamas make Emma look like a giant purple popsicle. She tells Emma this each time she wears them, but Emma just shrugs and laughs.

Along the side of the wall hang framed collages that Emma has made from photos. Clipped photos of Quinn and their parents and of the fish, Scales, Emma once had. Of school and friends and teams and dance recitals. Of vacations and birthday cakes and holidays. Quinn tried to make a collage of photos once, too. She gave up after cutting out three pictures.

The closet door is wide open. Clothes Quinn once wore that have passed to Emma now hang gathering dust. Quinn tries hard to picture Emma wearing each and every one. But it's difficult. Exactly how tall was Emma? Where did her hair last reach? Quinn panics. How long will it be before Emma's face gathers dust and fades into the gray closet of Quinn's memory?

She begins twisting the ends of her hair. Emma always did

that. She'd snuggle up to Quinn whenever she could, reach over, and start twisting her hair. Quinn would push Emma's hand away, but it always found its way back to Quinn.

Quinn's mother enters the room. She stretches across Quinn's bed and stares at the still life along with Quinn.

"I-I'm sorry," says Quinn quietly. She's cried a billion tears. She can't cry anymore. "It's my fault."

"Don't say that," says her mother, putting an arm around her shoulder. "No one blames you."

Quinn swallows hard. She wants to tell her mother everything—about what really happened that day after school. She stands and opens her mouth. She tries. But the words are too heavy. So heavy she can't lift them and force them out of her mouth. She stares at her mother with eyes filled with pain.

Her mother doesn't see. She looks past Quinn to the purple sleeve. She gets up and tucks it under Emma's pillow. She walks out of the room.

Quinn sinks back onto her bed, melting into the covers. She looks over at Emma's stuff. The orange backpack sits slumped against the wall so that its enormous smiley face is now more a wrinkled frown. She hears a tiny clink—like the breaking of fine glass. Another piece of her heart has snapped off.

Quinn's about to close her eyes when they settle on the book on Emma's nightstand—the book Emma hadn't had a chance to finish. She reaches over and picks it up. It falls open to the bookmarked page.

Slowly, carefully, she begins to read.

18

THERE WAS A SOFT KNOCK AT THE DOOR.

Kara sprang from the bed. "Mom! Dad!"

Quinn tried to hold her back in case it was the crazy man, but Kara was already opening it.

Persephone stood in the hallway, looking pleasantly into the room. "Hello, girls. I've come for Joe."

She extended her hand—a long, thin hand with that pale translucent skin that gave Quinn the creeps. Joe moved toward her.

Instinctively Quinn stretched out an arm to bar his path. "He's not going with you," she said firmly. "He's staying with us."

Then someone else appeared beside Persephone. It was

the old woman with cotton-candy hair and crinkly gray eyes. Quinn had seen her in the restaurant earlier that morning.

"Grandma?" shouted Joe, charging through Quinn's barrier, past Persephone. He threw himself into the old woman's arms. "But . . . ?"

"Time to go, Joey," she whispered, smoothing his hair, gripping him tightly.

Joe squeezed hard for a moment, and then drew back still holding her hands. "But . . . Adam?" he said softly.

Persephone exchanged glances with the old woman. They both smiled and nodded. "Adam is going to be fine," said the old woman. She looked at Kara and winked.

Joe hugged his grandmother again. He took a deep breath and smiled. He turned toward Quinn and Kara. "I have to go now. Thanks for helping."

Kara frowned. "What about *my* family? Where are *they*? When are they coming?"

"Don't worry," said Persephone. "I'm sure you'll see them soon."

Joe walked slowly alongside his grandmother and Persephone down the long dark corridor. Before they disappeared around the corner, Joe turned back. He lifted his hand and waved, and then he, too, was gone.

Quinn looked at Kara. "Something isn't right. I saw that

woman earlier. If she was here earlier why didn't she come for Joe? Maybe she isn't really his grandma. Maybe someone who looks like her."

"Let's follow them," said Kara.

"What about the man?" asked Quinn. "What if we run into him?"

"He's probably still pacing the hallway near Joe's room. Probably doesn't even know we've left. We'll keep an eye out."

Quinn agreed.

Kara locked the door and Quinn took her hand, gripping it tightly. Together they made their way through the hall toward the lobby.

When they got to the entrance, Quinn poked her head around the corner. An old woman moved with her walker toward the restaurant. A man was milling about at the front desk talking to Persephone. The guy with the ball cap wasn't there.

Neither was Joe. She wondered how Persephone had gotten him to his family and then returned to the front desk so quickly.

Then she heard the familiar grinding noise of the elevator cables. Through the metal bars she saw Joe, standing beside his grandmother.

The operator, Sharon, was saying, "Kindly place any hand baggage in the overhead bins. Larger pieces must be stowed beneath your seat."

Joe was looking up at his grandmother, smiling.

"There he is," said Kara. "I guess the rest of his family's waiting for him upstairs."

"Just like Mr. Mirabelli," said Quinn.

"Who?" asked Kara.

"The old man in the pajamas."

The windows of the hotel had turned to mirrors once again, which meant all remaining sunlight was gone. Quinn stared briefly into one mirror and then into another, as if the reflections might tell her something the real space couldn't. All they told her was that it was late. And she suddenly remembered they hadn't had dinner. She wasn't hungry, but they'd need to eat to keep up their strength. Something told her she'd need her strength.

Back in the room, Kara ordered a large pizza.

Quinn switched on the TV. She was greeted by fuzz. She flipped from channel to channel. Nothing. She hit the top of the TV a few times, hoping something would jog the connection, but nothing changed. She switched it off.

The pizza and pop arrived in no time. Neither of the girls had much appetite, but having something warm in their stomachs was a comfort. Quinn made sure both the dead bolt and the security chain were engaged. Then they washed up and got ready for bed.

"Let's sleep in our clothes," Quinn suggested.

"Why?" asked Kara.

Quinn didn't have a good answer. "Just in case," was all she could think of to say.

Kara seemed to ponder this for a moment and then nodded. She threw herself in the bed her mother had slept in. The bruises on her arms and legs had deepened in color. She rubbed her knee.

"I'm tired," she said, yawning. "Like I could close my eyes and sleep forever."

Quinn stretched across the other bed. "Me too." But she was afraid to sleep. Everyone kept disappearing. She was afraid if she closed her eyes—even for a moment—she'd lose Kara, too.

"Give me your hand," Quinn said suddenly. "The one with the bracelet."

Kara sat up and frowned. "This isn't the time for silly stuff."

"Come on. I'm not losing you, too."

Quinn untied the knot on her wrist. She slipped her band through Kara's, just as she'd done before. Together they retied it. They were linked once again so that, even asleep, neither could move without the other knowing.

"Forever?"

"Forever," said Kara. She took a deep breath and settled back into bed. After some time she spoke quietly. "Remember the time I got stuck in that tree in the forest behind the school?"

Quinn smiled.

"You wouldn't leave me. Not even to get help." Kara's voice was soothing and the memories calming. "You climbed up and then we were both stuck."

Quinn yawned. "Yeah. That was dumb."

"We got down. Eventually," said Kara.

"That's 'cause Emma found us. She was always trying to tag along."

Kara continued to talk. She spoke of good times. Things they'd done. Things they'd planned to do.

They lay there, on opposite beds, their arms dangling in the center. It wasn't comfortable, but Kara seemed weak and exhausted. As soon as she stopped talking she drifted off.

Quinn couldn't fall asleep. She couldn't stop thinking about Emma. What if Emma really was here? What if that freaky man was the guy who had abducted her? Maybe he somehow knew what Quinn looked like. What if he knew that Quinn knew the truth about who he was and that's why he was after her? What if he had Emma locked in some room?

Quinn managed to switch off the bedside lamp. Waves of exhaustion splashed over her as the events of the day unfolded in her mind. They were stuck in the middle of the desert, and no one knew they were there.

What if it was something entirely different? Maybe they'd stumbled upon some freak cult who preyed upon lost travelers. Perhaps they brainwashed people until they no longer knew who they were. She and Kara would wind up worshipping heads of lettuce, devoting themselves to snake-handling, and drinking from cups made from skulls of dead animals.

Or, perhaps Josh was right. Maybe Area 51 aliens *had* escaped. They'd set up shop in the desert and were collecting lost travelers, using them as specimens, experimenting with them.

A million strange ideas danced inside Quinn's mind, each more bizarre and horrific than the last. Finally, sleep rose up around her and she let herself sink beneath its inky surface.

The TV clicked on. Quinn's eyes snapped open.

She sat up and searched the room. For a moment she'd forgotten where she was, whether it was night or day. On the opposite bed, Kara breathed heavily, fast asleep. Their hands were still tethered by the bracelets. Quinn breathed a sigh of relief. Kara hadn't disappeared.

The TV drew her attention. Black-and-white fuzz filled the screen. Had someone turned it on? Impossible. They were alone.

Quinn swung her legs over the side of the bed and stood. She tried to reach for the power switch, but she was tethered to Kara's arm.

The swarming black dots on the screen gathered, drawn to each other like tiny magnets. They grew into dark clusters that began to take shape. Behind the shadows, the blue-white screen melted into color. The shapes grew clearer and a scene unfolded, as though someone had downloaded a movie and hit play.

19

The front of the school is dark. The pavement and lawn are covered with a thick layer of snow. People are gathered outside the building. They hold candles.

The scene is the vigil—the memorial they held for Emma.

The camera focuses on the Cawstons. All three lean into one another, as though only their combined effort can keep them upright. Mrs. Cawston holds a single white candle.

The camera shifts. It finds Quinn's mother and father standing a few feet away. They are marble statues, all pale and ghostly. Neither moves a muscle. A neighbor—Mrs. Johnston—hands Quinn's mother a bouquet. She accepts it mechanically.

The camera pans the crowd.

Most of the teachers have come. Mr. Mason's shoulders

sag. Ms. Giuliani's head is bent. Señora Márquez's body quakes. She sobs quietly, warm puffs of air lingering in the chill around her.

All the kids are there as well. Some hold hands. Some hug each other. Tears stream down some faces, dampening cheeks and collars.

Against the fence is a makeshift memorial. A girl from Quinn's class breaks free from the crowd. It's Becky Hewlet. She makes her way toward the fence and adds a small teddy bear to the growing pile of stuffed animals and flowers and cards and signs.

Quinn's mother begins to tremble. Her knees buckle. Mrs. Cawston releases Josh and Mr. Cawston and lunges for her. The two women bury their faces in each other's shoulder.

The camera rises to a bird's-eye view.

Quinn stares at the screen. Something is wrong. Something is missing.

Then slowly, bit by bit, the scene begins to transform. The snow melts and the grass on the lawn grows green and lush. The sky brightens, like an eerie reverse sunset.

All the people remain standing, fixed to their spots, their candles flickering softly, but their clothes have changed. Boots and heavy coats disappear, replaced with shorts and T-shirts.

It wasn't January . . .

Quinn's heart beat quicker. Panic swelled inside her chest. She didn't want to see any more of this movie. She stretched out her arm, dragging Kara along with her. But Kara was heavy, sound asleep.

She managed to get close enough to hit the power switch with the tip of her toe, but nothing happened. The movie continued.

The camera focuses on the fence. It zeroes in on the stuffed animals that surround a portrait.

Quinn jabbed the button again, this time harder.

The camera zooms in. Closer. Closer.

Quinn kicked wildly at the TV. She didn't care if she knocked it down. She dragged Kara farther and punched the button again and again with her fist, but the film continued.

The picture is out of focus, but the portrait fills the entire screen. The background grows dark around the edges and the darkness begins to eat up the portrait, with the image growing clearer by the second.

Quinn squeezed her eyes shut, but there was no stopping it. She couldn't erase what she'd seen. She crumpled into a heap beside Kara, trying desperately to breathe.

The portrait was not of Emma.

It was a portrait of Quinn and Kara.

20

KARA STIRRED. "What's wrong? Are my parents back? Josh?"

Quinn looked at Kara. Tears flowed down her cheeks. She struggled for air.

The TV was off. The film was done. A dead screen glared at her. She switched on the bedside lamp. The light hovered on the screen above her reflection like a halo.

Quinn's voice was low and trembling. "No. They're not. We have to leave. Now."

Kara sat up and searched the room. "What are you talking about? Why are you crying? What time is it?"

"Don't you get it?" said Quinn. "There's no time here." She swiped at her eyes with the back of her hand. "There are no clocks. No phones. No TV. This place is all wrong. We have to leave."

"Leave?" demanded Kara. "How can we leave? We're in the middle of the desert. And what about my parents? And Josh?"

Quinn took a deep breath. There were words she and her parents never spoke, words they were too afraid to say because if they said them it would make them real—those words were *Emma is never coming back.*

Now Quinn had new words stuck in the back of her mind—words her brain tried to block her mouth from saying. But, one by one, she forced them out.

"Your parents are not coming back. Neither is Josh. We have to leave, Kara. It's our only chance."

"But—"

"Listen," said Quinn. "Remember when I made Persephone look through the guest book for Emma?"

Kara nodded.

"Well," she continued, "I saw something. I saw our names all written out neatly—each of them—except your mom and dad's and Josh's were crossed out. Persephone crossed them out, Kara. Like they'd left. Checked out."

And she told Kara about the bloody pillow, the movie of the vigil. They were warnings. Omens. She and Kara were in great danger.

"I know you think I went crazy after Emma disappeared. I know you don't believe that I saw her here because I thought I saw her so many times before. But your parents wouldn't abandon us. Neither would Josh. There's something really wrong. We have to leave. Now."

Kara's lip quivered. She nodded slowly. "But . . . where will we go? We'll get lost. We'll die out there."

"The diner," said Quinn suddenly. "We'll backtrack to the diner. We'll follow the road to the interstate and we'll find the diner. There was a pay phone there, remember? And Not-Norm will help us. I'm sure he will."

They emptied the bottles of flat pop and filled them with water from the bathroom sink. They wrapped the remaining slices of pizza and packed them in a pillowcase. It wasn't much, but it was all they had—all they could think to bring along.

Quinn took a deep breath. "Now, we just need to get out of here."

With Kara still attached and the pillowcase slung over her back, Quinn slipped into the hall.

It was darker than usual—as though someone had dimmed the lights. Quinn wished she'd hear Joe's crying again. Even that would have brought her comfort.

Slowly, carefully, she and Kara crept down the hall. Except for Persephone, who lurked behind her counter, and

Sharon, who was leaning over speaking to her in hushed whispers, the lobby was deserted.

This was it. Their chance.

Quinn held a finger to her mouth and Kara nodded. They grasped each other's hand so the bracelets wouldn't cut if they pulled apart. They stepped lightly, careful not to make a sound. They were a few steps closer to the door when Quinn saw him at the opposite end.

He stood in the hall archway. His eyes zeroed in on Quinn and Kara and his forehead folded into a deep crease.

All blood drained from Quinn's face. She could feel it pooling somewhere near her chest, making it hard to breathe and harder to think.

"Hey!" he called. "Stop!"

Persephone and the elevator operator looked up. Their attention snapped first toward the man who was yelling and then toward Quinn and Kara.

Panic wrapped itself around Quinn's throat. They'd never make it to the front entrance and out the door in time—not with Aides standing guard.

Quinn's eyes swept right to left, searching for somewhere—anywhere—to run. That's when she saw it, wide open and waiting.

Kara must have seen it, too, because she yanked Quinn's hand and together they made for the old elevator.

Quinn sprang into the cramped cage, dropping the pillowcase of water and pizza at her feet, while Kara grabbed the exterior door with her free hand. It wouldn't budge. Frantically, she searched the wood panels but could find no keyhole and no key. Kara heaved and yanked with all her might but the door wouldn't move.

"Won't. Close," she grunted, tugging with all her strength.

All at once Quinn saw the release button on the floor. She jumped on it and the door flew shut, knocking Kara backward into the elevator.

Sharon lunged at them. "No!"

The crazed-looking man raced toward the elevator. "Stop! Wait!"

Kara had managed to grab the metal gate before slamming backward into Quinn.

Quinn reached for something to keep herself from falling. Her hand found the large lever protruding from a circular brass base. She gripped it tightly and the lever lurched. With a liquidy hiss, the hydraulics kicked in and the elevator began to move. Down.

Quinn released the lever. The elevator halted midfloor. She could still see Sharon, now crouched, looking at them through the opening at the top of the cage.

"No!" she called. "Not that way!"

Her pasty smile had morphed into a frantic frown. She looked worried. Really worried.

Quinn reached for the lever, but as she gripped it another face appeared in the opening.

The man wore a fierce scowl, making his already wild eyes appear maniacal. He grabbed the metal bars, his skin stretching white across his knuckles, as though he might rip the bars apart. He opened his mouth to say something, revealing a row of jagged, broken teeth.

Quinn's body reacted independently of her brain. She yanked the lever again. In an instant, the man, the elevator operator, and the lobby disappeared above their heads.

The floor fell out from under them as the elevator plummeted. Quinn released the lever and stumbled sideways, gripping the back rail. Even without her hand on the control, they continued to drop. But the car didn't rattle or sway. There was no friction on the hydraulic cables, no squealing or thrumming or grinding to indicate the elevator was broken. They were smoothly and silently racing downward.

Kara grabbed Quinn's arm. "What's happening?"

Quinn struggled to her feet and reached for the lever. She tried to push it in the opposite direction, but it wouldn't move. It was stuck. "This makes no sense! There can't be this many floors!"

"We're going to die!" shouted Kara. "We're going to be crushed when we hit the bottom."

It felt like there'd never be a bottom. Like they'd remain in the elevator dropping for eternity.

Quinn blinked back tears, searching desperately for an emergency button or a help phone, but there was neither.

It was her fault. She shouldn't have let the crazy man spook her.

Quinn hugged Kara. She wasn't going to let go. If this was the end—the very end—if they were going to be flattened like pancakes at the base of the elevator, at least they were going to be flattened together.

She buried her face in Kara's shoulder and braced for impact.

21

THE DOWNWARD MOMENTUM EASED. The pressure fell and the car slowed. And with a faint and final hiss, the elevator came to a complete and dead stop.

Quinn exhaled as though it was all over. She smiled faintly. Then she saw what Kara saw—what lay beyond the metal cage—and the smile slid from her lips.

The elevator had come to rest in darkness—a darkness so thick, so complete, that even the soft yellow glow of the elevator lamp could not illuminate more than a few inches.

"Wh-where are we?" asked Kara. She let go of Quinn, walked to the metal bars, and stared into icy silence. There was no door to the elevator shaft here. Just the metal bars that separated them from the emptiness that lay beyond.

"I-I dunno," said Quinn. Her breath was hot and the air frigid. Vapor puffed from each word. "Some kind of basement."

Quinn's voice echoed outward like sonar, giving her a sense of the vastness beyond. It was like they'd dropped into some giant pit. It made her think of Adam. And Joe. She hoped Joe was all right. She hoped the upper floors of the hotel were way nicer than the basement.

"Let's get outta here," muttered Kara, her voice magnified into a hoarse whisper by the echoing walls.

Quinn nodded and Kara stepped back from the gate. Quinn grasped the brass lever and tried to push it upward, but it was stuck. "Help me."

Kara grabbed the lever with both hands. Together they heaved and pushed and pulled, but it wouldn't budge. Not an inch.

"It's . . . broken . . ." Quinn grunted. They tried again and again, and then finally gave up.

Quinn left the lever and moved toward the metal gate. "What is this place?" she said in a breathy whisper. "A dungeon?"

Quinn slid open the creaky gate and poked her head deeper into the soupy darkness. The air was stagnant, like swamp water. The skin on her arms prickled. She hugged her chest.

"Hey!" she shouted at the ceiling of the elevator. "We're down here! Bring the elevator up!" She pounded at the side panels.

Kara joined in and together they screamed as loud as they could, hoping Persephone and the elevator operator could hear, hoping perhaps they were already trying to bring the car up. But nothing stirred.

"What are we going to do?" asked Kara.

Quinn tried the lever one more time. She kicked at it, but it wouldn't move. The thought of heading through a dark cave without even a little light was a horror all its own.

"Do you think there's a way out?" asked Kara.

"Hush," said Quinn suddenly.

"What?"

Quinn clamped a hand to Kara's mouth. "Listen."

Kara stared at the ceiling of the elevator. But the sound wasn't coming from above. It was coming from the darkness.

Quinn's body tensed as she strained to hear. Soft dripping, like a trickle of water falling on damp rocks. And then footsteps, lightly stepping on the wet, hard ground.

She was sure her mind was playing tricks again, but then she saw it—the faint flickering glow pushing its way through the cold gloom. Something was approaching.

Quinn grabbed Kara and yanked the metal gate shut.

They backed into the elevator until they were pressed against the rear paneling. Quinn snatched the pillowcase with the water bottles, and though it wasn't much of a weapon, she prepared to swing. They both stared, eyes wide, jaws limp.

As the flickering yellow light drew nearer, Quinn's imagination ran wild. What could possibly live in such a horrible place? A monster? A demon?

Something emerged from the black—something so completely unexpected it startled Quinn all the more.

Out of the shadows, lit only by the soft glow of the candle it held, was the small, delicate hand of a child. It grasped a brass saucer candleholder with the stub of a white twisted candle on top.

The girl was no older than six, wearing a long white nightie that draped to her dainty bare feet. Her yellow hair was matted and fell in scraggly waves over her shoulders. Her face was gaunt, her skin a ghostly white.

She stared at Quinn with gray expressionless eyes. Then she looked at Kara.

Her thin lips parted and she spoke in a tiny voice that was flat and watery, like the calm surface of a muddy pond.

"We weren't expecting you."

22

Quinn's sanity was held together with cobwebs. For the first time, she was certain she was losing her mind—if she hadn't already lost it.

The girl searched the inside of the elevator and frowned. "You've come alone."

"Where are we?" asked Kara.

The girl lowered her candle and stared at their wrists. "Is that comfortable? It doesn't look it."

"What kind of place is this?" said Quinn. "Who are you?"

The girl's eyes met Quinn's and a sliver of a grin snaked across her lips. She turned and walked silently back into the shadows.

"Hey, wait!" shouted Quinn. "Don't leave!" She lunged for the gate and slid it open. She chased after the girl, dragging Kara with her.

No sooner had they stepped outside the elevator than the gate sealed shut behind them. And in a flash so quick they didn't have time to turn, with a hideous grinding rush the elevator was gone.

Kara dove to catch it, but Quinn yanked her back. There was no door to this elevator; most likely it left behind an empty shaft. Something told Quinn if you fell into that, you'd fall forever.

The little girl glanced over her shoulder. "Come."

With the elevator gone, the glow of her candle seemed to grow stronger. It rippled outward, lighting the gloom, and Quinn was amazed at what she saw.

They were in a large room with a high, coffered ceiling, very much like the lobby of the hotel and yet completely different.

The floor was a glittering dark marble and the walls covered in pale yellow paper. The trim around the doors and archways was ornate, like the woodwork she'd seen with faces of people and animals carved into it. Only these looked like gargoyles—half human, half animal. Their colorless eyes appeared to follow her every move.

There was a counter, like the one Persephone stood behind. Only no one stood here and there were no keys and no dusty guest book.

Since they were deep below the ground, in place of windows there were tall framed mirrors. There were French doors on either end, immense leather armchairs, and heavy side tables with clawed feet. On several walls hung glassy-eyed animal heads—stags and bears and moose.

Kara squeezed Quinn's hand. She squeezed back. Quinn didn't want to follow the girl, but there was little choice. The girl had a candle and if there was a way out she would know it.

"Come," she repeated, her voice so thin. So sweet.

Quinn pulled Kara in close. "Do you think Emma could be down here?" she whispered.

Kara swallowed. "Or Josh?"

The thought had already occurred to Quinn. Josh was desperate to ride the elevator. It was possible he'd come to this place by accident like they had and couldn't get back up.

Quinn nodded grimly. Hugging each other, they caught up with the candle. It cast a lean shadow on the opposite wall that seemed to disentangle from them and dance about.

"Why is there no light down here? Electricity out?" Quinn asked.

"Yes," said the girl. "That's right."

"Where are you taking us?" said Kara. "Where are we going?"

Keeping her eyes fixed ahead, the girl giggled softly. "Why, the party, of course." There was something odd about her voice. Like unspoken things lingered just below the surface.

"Party?" said Quinn. "But we don't want to go to any party. We want to leave."

"Did you see a boy?" asked Kara. She held her hand above her head. "This high. Brown hair. His name is Josh?"

The girl shrugged. "Lots of boys come here. Lots of girls, too. I'm not sure."

Girls like Emma, thought Quinn. Perhaps this was the crazy dungeon where they kept all the abducted children. Now, more than ever, she was sure they had stumbled upon some kind of cult.

"If we go to your party," said Quinn, "will you show us the way out?"

The girl didn't respond. She kept walking. They had little choice but to follow. They crossed the great lobby, and then the girl held the candle toward the mouth of a dark hall.

"This way. Follow me."

She led them through a maze of intertwining halls. They twisted around a few times, descended steep steps, then continued. On either side were massive mahogany doors with no numbers.

"What's your name?" asked Kara suddenly.

The girl smiled. "It's difficult to pronounce. Most people don't get it right." She kept walking.

Quinn frowned at Kara. The sooner they got out of this weird place the better.

They continued along a narrow corridor. Quinn felt certain they were descending. Ahead, in the distance, a murmur echoed. It grew louder as they drew nearer. The little girl led the way through a series of archways and the noise became less fuzzy, the sounds more distinct. There was music and laughter and other party sounds.

"Here we are," she said, showing them through a final doorway.

They entered a vast room lit with dozens of flickering candles set upon tables surrounding a dance floor. The walls were dark wood paneling and the ceiling a giant mirror reflecting the people and the light.

A crowd danced in the center of the room to strange music. They shook and jittered and twisted and hopped, laughing and smiling and singing along like they knew each and every song by heart. They were having the time of their lives.

Quinn and Kara made their way around the tables to the opposite wall, where a huge buffet stretched the length of the room. Quinn's greedy eyes took it all in. There was every type of meat imaginable—lamb, ribs, turkey, chicken, and a whole pig roasting on a spit. Salads, rice, pasta, and potatoes filled bushel-size silver bowls. There were trays of pickles, dips, and hors d'oeuvres; apples sautéing in butter-brandy, fresh fruit, and mountains of desserts dripping with chocolate and cream. People piled their plates with all sorts of goodies.

"You see," said the little girl. "It's a grand party. We're so glad you could join us."

Quinn stood for a moment, searching the crowd for Emma and Josh. No one looked even vaguely familiar. Some of the dancers had wild grins on their faces, others were laughing uncontrollably. They wore strange clothes, from different time periods, as though this were some kind of costume ball.

Kara was searching, too. It was possible Josh and her parents were here, hidden somewhere in the crowd.

"Emma," muttered Quinn, searching each and every face.

She felt a cold hand touch her cheek. She looked down at the little girl, who—although a lot younger—suddenly reminded her of her sister.

"You can stay here," said the girl. "Stay with me. You can call me Emma, if you like. We can sing and dance and play forever."

Ice prickled Quinn's heart. Yes, she thought. I could stay here. Why not? It was a great place and everyone was having so much fun. And she and Kara would be together. Forever. Quinn would never have to return home to the neighbors who stared at her in silent pity, to the school where everyone talked around her in hushed whispers, where no matter what she did or said the teachers didn't give her bad grades anymore. Or to her parents—the people who seemed to forget she was hurting as much as they were.

"Shrimp?" said Kara, picking up a particularly fat one.

Quinn felt a drop on her head. Then another. And another.

She stepped aside and searched the mirrored ceiling for the leak. When she couldn't find one, she looked back at Kara's shrimp.

It was gray and alive and wriggling in her hand.

23

QUINN KNOCKED THE SHRIMP TO THE GROUND.

"Hey!" said Kara. "Why'd you do that?"

Quinn felt another drop. Above her the ceiling began to swish and swirl. It wasn't a great mirror at all, but dark, swampy water, like a giant murky pool.

She watched in horror as a black, wraithlike shadow scaled the far wall. It dove into the water ceiling and glided the length of the pool, one end to the other. Quinn recognized its shape immediately—it was what she'd seen swimming at the bottom of the hotel pool.

The pools were connected. The bottom of one was the top of the other. Something lived between the two worlds.

Whatever it was, it could reach up and drag unsuspecting swimmers down.

Quinn's head began to spin. Nothing here was what it appeared to be. She stared wide-eyed at the little smiling girl. She was not Emma. She was nothing like Emma.

Quinn grabbed hold of Kara and steadied herself. Then everything else around her began to transform.

The music, once fun and melodious, had no rhythm, no tone. It was like metal grinding on metal. It hurt her ears. She cupped them, pulling up Kara's hand with hers, but she couldn't block it out.

The people continued to dance, but now Quinn saw they weren't a fun, happy crowd at all. They looked more and more like a frenzied mob, their movements angular and awkward, like wooden marionettes with someone pulling their strings.

On their faces, what Quinn had thought were smiles were grimaces of pain. What she believed to be laughter was actually screams of agony. It was like someone was forcing them to dance. To dance and dance and never stop.

The buffet changed as well. The pickles turned into slugs, and the rice into a pile of wriggling maggots. The meat she had thought looked delicious was moldy green and rotting, and she was sure that what looked like potatoes was an entirely different horror.

But all this didn't seem to sway the guests, who filled their plates with the disgusting, decaying food. They stuffed their faces mouthful after mouthful like they, too, couldn't stop.

Quinn watched as one woman bit off the head of a shrimp and ground the shell between her teeth. A man shoveled a spoonful of maggots into his mouth, strays dripping from his lips and crawling down his chin.

Quinn's stomach lurched. She was going to be sick. The only thing stopping her from collapsing into a heap was one single, all-important thought—they had to get out of this place. Right away.

She grabbed Kara's hand and pulled her close. She wasn't sure if Kara could see what she saw. "Don't touch anything," she hissed. "And don't say a word."

The little girl eyed Quinn and Kara. In the glow of her candle, she smiled a wide smile, and for the first time Quinn could see her little teeth were yellow and razor-sharp and her lips and tongue were black as night. She giggled. It was the most chilling sound Quinn had ever heard.

Without thinking, Quinn snatched the candle from the girl's hand and, gripping Kara, sprinted for the door. She raced through the crowd, weaving in between the crazy guests, who bumped and slammed into them as they tried to pass.

"Wait. Don't leave. The party's just getting started." The little girl's airy voice echoed over the music.

They ran without looking back, through archway after archway, until they reached a corridor that seemed to lead upward. Everything around them had changed as well. Quinn knew when she heard Kara gasp that she was beginning to see it, too.

The doors in the hallway were not mahogany—they were rusted cast iron. Loud banging filled Quinn's ears—people screaming, desperate to get out. Some doors opened a crack, as if held back by chains. Scabbed and bloody arms reached out, clawing for them.

Kara stifled a scream and pressed herself close to Quinn. Together they wove though various passageways, around and around, up one section and down the next, through one crossroads and then another. They ran for some time but did not reach the lobby.

Quinn came to a dead stop, bending over to catch her breath.

"We're lost," said Kara between gulps of air.

The candle flickered in Quinn's trembling hand. She stared at Kara and nodded. Then over her shoulder she saw it. Beyond the endless rattling doors and the clawing hands, glowing in the darkness was a pair of yellow eyes. It was the ghostly girl and she was moving toward them at a steady pace.

Frantically Quinn pulled Kara toward the opposite end,

but just beyond the candle's glow stood a shape, etched out of darkness. Quinn's heart jammed so far up her throat she could scarcely utter a sound. One word squeezed from her tight lips. "Him!"

At the opposite end of the corridor stood the man with the ball cap. He'd managed to find them and was running toward them. Quinn stood frozen to the spot, searching one way, then the other.

The glowing eyes had grown larger and the girl emerged from the darkness, her white gown fluttering in tatters around her, and stretched out her tiny hands. She was inches away, about to dig her claws into Kara, when Quinn felt herself being scooped up, lifted into the air by a big, muscled arm that wrapped itself around her waist. She had no voice to scream. Instead she hung there, clinging to the candle. Kara flopped beside her like a rag doll as the man carted them off at lightning speed.

The candleholder slipped from Quinn's hand, but Kara managed to scoop it up before it fell to the ground. Finally, they burst through the last archway and were back in the main lobby.

The front desk was bleak and decayed. And the frames of the French doors were sagging, the glass cracked. The knobs and hinges were streaked with rust. The animal heads—

now mutations, with horns and eyes where there shouldn't be—squealed and cried.

Mold grew like thick black blankets, draping from parts of the ceiling and walls. Between the sheets of fungus were clusters of mushrooms, some with caps as big as Quinn's hand. Like a hideous wave rolling toward them, the mold was spreading quickly. If they didn't get out soon, they'd drown in it.

"Look!" said Kara, aiming the candle toward the end of the lobby.

A doorway of soft light had slid open in the wall. It was the elevator, and Sharon was motioning for them.

"Hurry!" she shouted. "Move!"

The huge man bolted toward the elevator, carrying Quinn and Kara. The little girl's laughter echoed throughout the lobby. She moved toward them with feet that no longer touched the ground.

The man dove into the metal cage, still holding the girls. He dropped them and Kara tossed the candle out into the darkness. It exploded in a fiery ball as the gate sealed shut and the elevator kicked into motion.

Quinn shuddered. The pale face with the sharp teeth and black lips disappeared into the flames, her voice still ringing in Quinn's ears.

"Come back anytime. I'll be waiting."

Sharon looked at them and sighed. "You shouldn't have come here."

"What kind of place was that?" yelled Quinn.

"And what was that . . . *thing*?" said Kara.

Sharon looked deeply and steadily into Quinn's eyes and then Kara's. Quinn could tell the woman was genuinely concerned.

"Some questions are best left unanswered," said Sharon.

Quinn and Kara stood closer as the elevator zipped up what felt like only a floor or two. The man gripped Quinn's wrist.

The pillowcase filled with the rest of the pizza and the water bottles still sat in a heap on the floor of the elevator where Quinn had dropped it. She eyed Kara, then the pillowcase. Kara understood immediately. Kara picked it up and slung it over her shoulder.

They weren't done running.

24

PERSEPHONE STOOD OUTSIDE the elevator. As soon as Sharon slid open the iron gate Persephone began scolding them.

"What were you two thinking? Do you have any idea?" Her eyes were wide and her hair a mess. She looked frazzled and wild. It was the first time she wasn't wearing her perfect smile.

Quinn looked up into the crazy man's eyes. He still clutched her wrist. She exchanged glances with Kara. Kara's chin bobbed once, letting Quinn know she was ready. She was focused. It was time to leave Inn Between.

Kara swung the pillowcase with all her might, striking the man on the side of the head. He let go of Quinn and yelped. Together they pushed past Persephone, making a beeline for the front door.

"Stop!" shouted Persephone.

"Wait!" said Sharon.

Aides was standing outside, but luckily he was facing away. Quinn grabbed the pillowcase from Kara in case she needed it. She tucked her chin and burst through the door, bulldozing past the huge man before he had a chance to react.

"Hey!" he shouted. "Come back!"

"You can't leave!" yelled Persephone, who had reached the door. "You can't leave yet!"

Side by side, Quinn and Kara ran blindly into the dark desert dust. They followed the path that led away from the hotel. All the while the pillowcase thumped against Quinn's back like a sledgehammer. Running with their hands tied was awkward, but she and Kara were a team, and they managed to train their crazy legs and get their bodies to move as one.

Persephone, Aides, and Sharon kept calling for them to return. But Quinn ignored their calls and continued to run until she and Kara were swallowed by darkness. The voices faded into the distance.

"Keep . . . going . . ." breathed Quinn. "We . . . can't stop . . . until . . . we're sure they're not coming."

But Kara was slowing.

The hotel with its lit windows and high roof disappeared behind hills of gravel and rock. Ahead, the orange sun was sneaking over the horizon. They'd be easy to spot in daylight.

Quinn kept checking over her shoulder. There was no one there, but she just couldn't push the idea from her mind—something had followed her out of the hotel.

The farther they got, the stronger Quinn felt. They were going to be okay. They would make it to the diner, and Not-Norm would help.

"The bracelet—" breathed Kara. "It's cutting into my skin. Can we take them off?"

Quinn could see crisscrossed rings of bright red wrap around Kara's wrist. She remembered the dull aching pain all too well.

Surprisingly there were no such rings around her own wrist. "No. Not until we're safe. We need to stick together and it's the only way to be sure."

"But we're away from the hotel," said Kara. "We're okay now."

Kara was right. But it all seemed too easy. Like Persephone and Aides had let them go. Quinn wouldn't feel safe until they reached the interstate. Maybe not until they were back at Not-Norm's and calling the police.

They slowed to a brisk walk. Quinn stared gloomily at the alien landscape—the bleak mounds of rolling gravel. The rising sun melted over the terrain and the dust began to glisten gold again. Patches of creosote appeared, telling Quinn they were getting closer to the interstate.

Kara rubbed her wrist. The skin was breaking. The bruises on her arms had spread. In the morning light, her face seemed pale and her eyes dark and sunken. Quinn wondered if she looked as bad as Kara. She didn't feel bad, though. In fact, she felt pretty good. Better and better by the minute.

"I need some water," said Kara. "Just a sip."

Quinn took out one of the pop bottles they'd filled with water and they each had a sip. It was lukewarm and tasted like medicine. Maybe it was Quinn's imagination, but she thought it smacked of mold.

"No one's following us," said Kara. "They'd have caught us by now. Let's stop for a rest. Just a short one."

Kara was right. If they had been chased by a car, the girls would have been caught by now. Even if they had been pursued on foot, with their hands tied they'd have been no match. Still, Quinn couldn't shake the feeling she hadn't seen the last of Inn Between.

They left the path and climbed over a huge rocky hill. Tucked safely on the other side, they sat for a rest. With the sun beating down, the creepy crawlies had slunk back into hiding. Still, Quinn kept a sharp eye out for anything slinking or slithering.

"What happened to my parents? To Josh?" said Kara. "Where did they go?"

"I don't know," said Quinn. "But Persephone was right about one thing. You'll see them soon. I'm sure of it."

Quinn pulled Kara to her feet. "Come on. We have to keep going."

They walked for hours, easing along the gravel road. The heat hit them from both ends—the sun pressed down from above and the sand from below. Quinn could feel her body beginning to boil.

They'd taken a few more sips of water, emptying one of their two reserves. Kara was getting weaker. Though Quinn felt surprisingly strong, it took all her strength to hold Kara upright.

It was past noon when they settled into the pizza. Though it tasted like cardboard, Quinn chewed her slice, making each mouthful count. Just the thought of the disgusting buffet made the old pizza seem like a treat.

The hills began to look alike. Quinn searched the distance for any sign of the interstate. She saw none. By late afternoon, Kara had reached her end.

"I can't go on any farther," she said. "I need to rest."

They settled down for a short break in a thin patch of shade behind a hill. Kara rubbed her wrist and ankle.

They sat for some time in silence. The sun was beginning to descend. The ride in from the interstate to the hotel hadn't seemed this long, though Quinn recalled they'd circled around a few times. Still, by her calculations they must have walked over ten miles already. The last two or so had been slow going. Kara needed to stop frequently, and Quinn let her rest. Though she kept a suspicious eye out, nothing was following them. At least nothing Quinn could see.

Kara closed her eyes while Quinn kept watch. Far off in the distance, black dots circled. Turkey vultures. Just what they needed. Quinn watched their swaying, swooping motion, just to make sure they weren't going to dive-bomb them again. Their movement was relaxing. Kara had fallen asleep. The evening air cleared Quinn's head. It smacked of rain, though there wasn't a cloud in sight. The creosote, Quinn thought, as she inhaled deeply. She closed her eyes and was drifting off, too. But then she heard it and startled awake.

It was back. The hum.

25

QUINN SHOOK KARA GENTLY. "Wake up. Time to go." But Kara didn't respond and her eyes stayed shut. Panic zipped through Quinn's veins. She shook harder. "Kara. Come on. Please."

Kara's eyelids fluttered and opened. She looked at Quinn and smiled, but then her eyes clouded over. It was like she couldn't focus. Like she was looking past Quinn at some distant point beyond.

"I feel thin," said Kara. "Like smoke. Like I could blow away."

"Don't say that," said Quinn. "Please don't."

The look in Kara's eyes frightened Quinn. It was the same look she'd seen in the face of the old man in pajamas.

In Joe before he rode the elevator. Kara was fading fast and there was nothing Quinn could do to stop it.

"I can't lose you, Kara. You're all I have left."

"Go get help," said Kara.

"I'm not leaving you. You're going with me. Or I'm staying. Just like that time in the tree." Quinn tried to drag Kara to her feet. "Come on. We're close now. Can't you hear it? Can't you hear the hum?"

The last time Quinn had heard the hum they were on the interstate, heading into the bright lights. It meant they must be close to the road. Close to the diner.

"Kara," said Quinn, tugging at her arm. "You can do it. We're almost there."

Twilight had cast its spell over the landscape. The air was the same hazy gold it had been when they'd seen the bright lights. Soon it would be dark and the beautiful yellow-orange sphere of the sun would be swallowed by the horizon.

Quinn shaded her eyes. That's when she saw him.

Silhouetted against the disk of the setting sun, a shadow rose. Quinn had to squint, but there was no mistaking him—the crazy man with the ball cap. He'd followed them. He'd found them. A small animal sound escaped her lips.

She mustered her strength and found her voice. "Get up!" she hissed. "We have to run. Now!" She pulled Kara to her feet. They took a few steps then stopped. Kara collapsed like dead weight. Quinn pulled with all her might and managed to get Kara back on her feet.

The man walked toward them steadily, drawing nearer by the second, bearing down on them like a bulldozer.

"Stop," he snarled.

Quinn managed to get Kara moving again. They weren't fast, but they hobbled as best they could along the path. The interstate was just ahead. Quinn could see a piece of it around the bend. If they could just make it to the road, someone would see them. Some car would stop and they'd be saved.

All the while, the hum grew louder and louder in Quinn's ears. It nearly drowned out the man's yelling. It sounded like an engine—a diesel engine getting closer and closer.

"Wait!" the man yelled.

Quinn didn't hear him. All she heard now was the hum. All she saw was the road—getting closer. She pulled Kara with all her strength and together they made it to the shoulder of the interstate.

Headlights approached. Quinn could see the bright beams coming straight out of the burning sunset. Something was headed toward them, toward Norm's Diner. If they could just catch a ride they'd get there. This was their chance.

Quinn slipped her arm under Kara's. She had to get to where the vehicle could see them. She had to stop it.

Whatever it was, it approached at high speed. The lights grew blindingly bright and Quinn had to shield her eyes. The closer it got, the louder the hum became. Whatever was coming toward her was the source. The source of the bright lights. And the hum.

She stepped out into the middle of the road, dragging Kara along with her. She waved frantically with her free arm, hoping to get the driver's attention, hoping he or she would see the two girls and stop.

As it drew closer, Quinn could see it clearly. A huge eighteen-wheeler—fully loaded, thundering toward her. She let go of Kara and waved wildly, flapping both her hands, along with Kara's, so hard she thought they might just take flight. The driver had to see them. There was no way he couldn't.

The truck was only half a block away when Quinn realized something was wrong. Its speed wasn't changing. It wasn't slowing down. Instead, it barreled toward Quinn and Kara at lightning speed, heading straight for them. Straight at them.

Quinn shut her eyes as the light enveloped her entire body and the sound exploded in her mind. The truck was going to hit them head-on.

26

QUINN HUGS HER ARMS to her chest. Her cheeks flush scarlet. Embarrassment and anger battle inside her.

"I have to stay late," she says, biting off each word.

Emma stares. Her shoulders sag. "Why? What'd you do?"

"Never mind," snaps Quinn. Her voice lashes like the November wind. "I just have to."

Emma sighs. She lets her orange backpack—the one with the huge smiley face—slip from her shoulder. It thunks to the ground by her once-white-now-gray sneakers. "I'll wait for you."

Kara is hurrying to catch her bus.

Quinn grabs her arm. "Sorry," she mutters.

Kara casts Quinn a withering glare. "You should never have asked me."

"Kara," says Quinn, but Kara's already rushing to make her bus. "I'll call you," Quinn yells after her.

Other kids from Quinn's class walk past. They look at Quinn. Some whisper. Some giggle.

Tears burn at the back of Quinn's eyes. She frowns hard and licks her dry lips. She wants to yell—tell them not to gawk, not to be so nosy. Instead, her anger forms a fine point. It flies like an arrow toward Emma.

"Go home." She digs the house key from her pocket and holds it out.

Emma draws back. "I can't walk by myself. Neither can you." She's wringing the pink cap in her hands, twisting it tighter. Tighter.

"Don't be such a chicken. Just go home." Quinn thrusts the key into Emma's hand.

"This isn't a good idea," says Emma, refusing to close her fingers on it. "You know the rule—we have to walk together."

"No one's gonna know," snaps Quinn. "Not if you don't say anything."

Emma shifts from side to side. "How long will it take you? I can wait by the office doors. I'll sit right here. Or—I can wait on the climber in the park."

Anger and frustration explode from Quinn. "I don't want

you to wait for me, okay? I'm tired of you always hanging around me. Can't you do anything by yourself?"

A hurt look washes over Emma. She deflates like a leaky beach ball. Her fingers curl slowly around the key.

She waits a moment longer, as if hoping Quinn will change her mind. When Quinn says nothing, she places her cap on her head, picks up her backpack, and slings it over her shoulder. With one last look at her sister, she turns and walks away.

The sun is fiercely bright. Quinn squints as she watches Emma head through the parking lot and onto the sidewalk.

She is suddenly sorry. She wants to call Emma back. She wants to yell Don't go! *but another group of sneering kids pass her.*

Quinn watches as Emma's pink cap moves farther and farther through the crowd, until it disappears into the blazing sunset.

She dives forward, but she can't move. The light is too bright. It stabs at her eyes. She struggles wildly. Her heart thuds in her chest.

Emma! I'm sorry!

There's nothing but light now. Pure white light. It wraps itself around Quinn. It squeezes the last breath from her lungs.

Emma! Come back!

Emma . . .

I love you!

27

A ROARING WHOOSH tore through Quinn's body as the vehicle flew past her. Flew through her. As though it were a great and powerful metallic ghost.

Quinn's eyelids fluttered. Before the ghost truck disappeared, leaving her standing helplessly in the middle of the deserted road, she'd caught sight of something that wrenched her thoughts, twisting them into a giant ball of confusion.

In the same instant, hands grabbed her shoulders and yanked. She tumbled onto the side of the road, rolling to a stop with Kara practically on top of her.

She felt his shadow before she saw him. He loomed over her, sharp features, glaring eyes. The image shattered her mind, smashing it to a billion pieces that drizzled down around her and fell to the dust like the tiny shimmering shards of a dream.

"I've been looking for you," said the man.

Quinn drew Kara in close, shielding her with her arms, as if looking at him might turn them both to stone. "You're not here. You can't be."

He continued as though he hadn't heard her, his voice breathy and tired. "I had to find you. I had to tell you all. I needed you to know."

Inch by inch, Quinn backed away. Somehow she had to get control of herself. She had to get Kara to her feet. Get her away from this man. From this . . . *ghost*.

"I never meant for it to happen." His words were so thick he had to choke them out. "I swear it. I never meant—"

"Get away from us," said Quinn. "You're not here. You can't be." Her thoughts scrambled this way, then that, desperate to cling to anything that made sense. How could this man be standing in front of her when he was driving the truck—the truck with the blinding lights and the engine with the hum so loud it nearly split her brain? How could he be in two places at the same time?

"Please," he said.

Quinn paused long enough to look into his eyes. And for the first time, they didn't seem crazy. Instead, they were filled with a sort of anguish—a deep and powerful pain tangled and mangled and mashed up with grief, a feeling Quinn understood all too well.

"Please," muttered the man, extending an arm. "Forgive me."

Quinn scrambled to her feet and heaved Kara up with all her might. Slowly, they backed away. "Leave us alone."

Quinn turned, and with Kara leaning into her, they hobbled in the direction of the diner. In the direction the ghost truck had fled.

"No," said the man, following them. "Don't go there. Not that way. You don't want to see."

Quinn ignored him and kept walking. Her world had shifted. It was not the same place it had been a moment ago. She knew now this man had no power over her. He was not what she'd thought he was. He couldn't hurt her. And he couldn't stop her.

They neared the top of the hill and froze. In the distance, Quinn heard it—a blast of horn, a screeching of brakes, and engines colliding in a sickening clash of metal on metal. And then nothing. Silence. The hum had exploded and then stopped. The vacuum it left had sucked all the sounds of the world along with it.

Quinn hugged Kara and forced her to move. She had to get to the top of the hill. She had to look down, to see it with her own eyes. If she didn't, she'd never know it was real.

The man kept pace, a few steps behind. "I was tired," he muttered, his voice soft and low, as if he were telling some long-forgotten tale. "My son had just gotten the diagnosis. I was trying to spend as much time at the hospital as I could, but we needed the money so I had to work. I was so tired. I wanted to stop. I called dispatch but the guy told me to get a cup of coffee, walk around the truck, and then keep driving. He said the tomatoes wouldn't keep—that I had to get them to the warehouse in Salt Lake City by morning. I told him I wasn't safe to drive, that I needed to rest. Just a few hours. But he said that wasn't the way the company rolled. He said I'd lose an entire week's pay if those tomatoes spoiled. We needed the money. I should have stopped. But the tomatoes . . ."

His words faded to a whimper. There was no threat left in him. Nothing about him could frighten Quinn anymore. She should have felt better, safer, only now a new fear spilled toward her—something much worse. What would she find if she looked down? What was at the base of the hill?

The silence was so thick it was strangling. Step by step, she moved upward, gasping for air. The last sliver of sunlight was fading from the sky. In the patches of deep purple and blue, Quinn could see black dots circling, swooping. Turkey vultures.

Then the silence was broken. Sirens came from both directions, converging on the spot. They frightened the birds, scattering them to the wind.

"What's happening?" asked Kara. "Where are we going?"

Quinn didn't answer. She just pulled Kara forward, each step heavy and painfully slow, until they reached the edge of the hill. Summoning every ounce of courage in her, Quinn looked down, silent witness to the chaotic scene below.

Kara's parents were there. Her father was on a stretcher, eyes open, wearing an oxygen mask. One paramedic attended to him, while two others bandaged Mrs. Cawston's head. Josh was on a stretcher as well. He was awake and his mouth was moving. He was alive and talking. They were all alive.

Kara's mouth opened but no sound came out. She straightened herself, taking it all in. "Look," she said softly.

Quinn followed her gaze to where she and Kara lay on the road. Paramedics were trying to revive them, but it didn't look hopeful. It was the last piece of an intricate puzzle. It was the reason why they were still here, why Mr. and Mrs. Cawston and Josh were not.

Kara's eyes filled with tears. "Forever?" she said in a choked whisper.

Quinn gripped her hand. "Forever," she echoed.

"Untie them!" shouted one paramedic to another, and a woman quickly severed the friendship bracelets—the threads that had kept Quinn and Kara bound together.

Quinn looked at her wrist. The ghost bracelets were still tied—a bond forged by so many shared moments. So much laughter, so many tears. Words that never needed to be spoken and thoughts exchanged without uttering a single sound. No scissors made of metal could cut this tie.

"You won't leave me, right?" said Kara. "No matter what?"

Quinn drew Kara in close and hugged her. She would not lose Kara like she'd lost Emma. No matter what it meant, no matter what the cost, she wouldn't make the same mistake.

"It was my fault," Quinn said, her voice trembling under the weight of the words she lifted one by one from her conscience. She heaved them out into the open air of the desert's fading sun, like dirty laundry she'd washed clean and hung to flap on a line for the world to see. "I'm the one who made her go home alone. Emma is gone because of me."

Kara lifted a pale, withering hand. She placed it gently on Quinn's shoulder.

"She wanted to wait for me," said Quinn, sobs filling the gaps between her words. "She said . . . she said she should wait, but I was so angry—at myself—at everyone—it all rushed out at Emma and I couldn't stop myself. I told her to go. I told her I didn't need her. I called her a chicken. And she left school alone because of me. She was stolen because of me."

Hot tears spilled down Quinn's cheeks. Tears of pain. Of longing. Of frustration. And hatred. Hatred for the person who had taken Emma. And hatred for herself for what she'd done. For what she could never take back.

Kara pulled Quinn toward her. She shook her head. "It wasn't you." Her chest heaved in and out in ragged breaths as she sobbed out her story. "It was me. I'm the one. I should never have given you my assignment. I should have said no to you when you asked me. If only I'd had the courage to say no to you, none of this would have happened. Don't you see? It's my fault, not yours."

Quinn swept a hand bitterly across her burning cheeks. She stared at Kara. Kara had been harboring the same horrible feeling—that Emma was gone and she had caused it. "It's not your fault. You couldn't have known."

Over her shoulder Quinn saw them. First Persephone and Aides. They joined the man, standing shoulder to shoulder with him, staring thoughtfully, silently, at the two friends. Then the three parted like a curtain, revealing another figure, a small form swathed in twilight. She was still wearing her fall jacket, the pink cap perched upon her head.

Quinn gasped. She sprang to her feet, leaping toward the figure, the name exploding from her lips. "Emma!"

Quinn pulled frantically, but something was holding her to the spot. Not allowing her to move forward, to reach Emma.

"Kara! Get up! Look! It's Emma! Don't you see? It's Emma!" But Quinn could get no closer to the golden silhouette shimmering in the dusk—Kara was dragging Quinn back.

Quinn slipped an arm under Kara, but she had grown too weak to stand.

"Emma!" shouted Quinn, waving wildly. "I told them I saw you! I knew it was you! You were here all along! You came for me! I knew it!"

She struggled to pull herself and Kara closer to Emma. How she'd dreamed of the day she'd see her again—all the things she'd tell her. All the things she'd say. Beginning with sorry. Sorry for what she did—for cheating on her assignment. Sorry for all the things she'd said, for saying that she didn't need Emma, because she did need her. Oh, how she needed her. She hadn't wanted Emma to leave. Not really. She loved her. Her heart ached to fly to Emma's side, to fly into her arms like a bird.

She stopped struggling.

Not-Norm's warning whispered in her memory. He said

he'd dreamed of a two-headed bird. Half the bird was trying to fly. The other half was bound to the ground. She gazed at her best friend—the deep bruises had spread over her body, the hollow circles had deepened around her eyes. They were that bird, she and Kara. Quinn wanted to fly, but Kara was broken. Kara was preventing Quinn from flying away.

"Let Kara go," said Emma, reaching out a beckoning hand. "It's time."

"No," whispered Kara, her eyes wide with horror. "Don't listen to her, Quinn. I'm not going anywhere. I'm not leaving you. Not ever."

"You have to, Quinn," said Emma. "It's the only way."

Quinn volleyed glances from Emma to Kara to the paramedics below. Then, like some tiny object way off in the distance that grows larger and clearer until you can finally make out its true shape, Quinn realized she'd gotten it all wrong. Kara wasn't the broken one. She wasn't the one holding Quinn back. It was Quinn that was broken. It was Quinn keeping Kara from returning.

She stared at Kara with watery eyes. She spoke softly. "You have to go back."

"No," sobbed Kara, shaking her head. "Don't do it, Quinn. I won't go. Just like the tree. If you stay, so do I."

Quinn looked at Emma. And then with trembling hands

she began to pick at the knot. The threads were coming loose, but with all her remaining strength Kara pushed her hand away.

"You promised you'd never leave me," whispered Kara, gripping Quinn's hand so tight the tiny bones threatened to break. "Forever? Don't you remember?"

Tears spilled down Quinn's cheeks. "Think of your parents, Kara. And Josh. Think of how much they'd miss you. And think of Joe's brother. Who will save Adam?"

"Adam?" said Kara.

Quinn pulled the final thread free. And then she grabbed both of Kara's hands, looking deep into her eyes. "We promised we'd help Adam. You have to go back now. You have to wake up. You have to be the one to tell them."

In the background, Quinn could hear the paramedics shouting more frantic instructions. She didn't notice if they were about her or about Kara.

"But," sobbed Kara, "will you . . . will you come back, too?"

Quinn thought about this for a moment. She looked down at the paramedics trying to revive her. Kara's parents had left Inn Between because they'd returned. So had Josh. Now it was Kara's turn. Would she be next? All that time they'd spent in Inn Between had been seconds of real time. Or no time at all. Could she go back, too? She looked at Persephone, who gazed at her steadily. Then at Emma. Then back at Kara. She smiled. "Maybe."

Kara's grip tightened. "Please, Quinn."

Quinn continued to smile, but this time she made no promise. "You have to go back now, Kara, it's your turn, they're losing you." Below, the paramedics had brought out a defibrillator and were attaching it to Kara. "I have to return to the hotel. My time there isn't up."

They gripped each other one last time and then let go. A strange lightness drifted over Quinn, as Kara faded from her grasp like smoke in the wind. In that same instant, Quinn heard a paramedic below.

"I have a pulse!" he yelled.

28

QUINN RACED TOWARD EMMA and flung her arms around her. She buried her head in Emma's shoulder and hugged her with all her might. She was in a field of bluebells.

Quinn smiled until her jaw ached. "It's you," she kept saying. "It's really you."

Emma smiled and nodded. She twisted a lock of Quinn's hair. They stood staring at each other for the longest time, and then they hugged again, holding each other as though they'd never let go. Time stretched into one long unbreakable moment that ended only when Persephone spoke.

"It's time," she said. She was waiting with Aides and the truck driver. But Quinn shook her head. She wasn't ready. Not yet.

Still gripping Emma's hand, Quinn turned to face the scene unfolding below. Kara had opened her eyes. She ripped the oxygen mask from her mouth and screamed when she saw Quinn.

Two paramedics tried to calm Kara as she struggled to get up, to reach for Quinn. One paramedic was trying to get the oxygen mask back over her mouth, but Kara pushed her hand away. She was still screaming Quinn's name.

"They're trying to revive her," said a paramedic. "You have to let them do their job."

"Come on, Kara," whispered Quinn. "Think of Adam. Remember Adam." Quinn closed her eyes and willed her thoughts through the invisible barrier of life and death.

When she opened her eyes, Kara had stopped struggling. Slowly, her mouth moved as if talking to herself. Then she grabbed the paramedic's arm. Quinn watched her lips form the sounds.

"Adam," she was saying. "I know where the missing boy is."

The paramedic stared at her. He tried to get an oxygen mask over her mouth but she pushed it away. Kara's lips kept moving. She kept talking. She was pointing. She would make them understand. Quinn knew she would. Adam would be okay. They'd find him and he'd be rescued. Joe could rest now.

In one hand, Quinn held the faded orange and purple bracelet that had bound her to Kara. She stared at the frayed threads that had held strong through so much. It was like a souvenir of another life. Not-Norm had said that once the spirit passes beyond, the people around here gave their names back to the desert. Quinn was not ready to give back her name, but she would give the desert something else.

Slowly, she bent down and lifted a small rock. A scorpion scuttled out from beneath, stared at her with black beady eyes, then ambled off to find other shelter. Quinn was no longer afraid of snakes and scorpions.

Gently, she scooped out a handful of dry soil. She tucked the bracelet into the hole and replaced the rock, patting it once.

The truck driver stood a few paces away, watching her. When Quinn looked up, he seemed tired and worn, like an old piece of tissue someone had balled up and tossed away. Back at the scene Quinn heard a paramedic pronounce him dead.

Quinn thought about what he'd said. He had a sick child. He wasn't in his right mind. He wasn't a bad man. He'd just done a bad thing. There was a difference. And he'd gone down into the basement of the hotel, into that horrible place, to help Kara and her. He'd risked himself to save them.

Still holding Emma with one hand, Quinn stretched the other out toward the man. He looked at it for a moment, and then placed his hand in hers. He smiled, and together with Emma, Persephone, and Aides, they walked back to Inn Between.

The return journey was short. They glided over the sand and gravel, their feet barely touching the ground. A lone coyote wailed in the distance at the hunter's moon hanging orange in the sapphire sky. Creosote saturated the air with the scent of falling rain.

When Quinn saw the hotel ahead—its windows all alit—she was strangely comforted. It was a good place after all. A cozy shelter where you could rest up for a while before you continued along on your journey—wherever that might be.

Aides swung the heavy wooden door open and held it as Persephone led the way inside. She gazed at Quinn with deep, thoughtful eyes, and then she smiled and her smile didn't seem phony at all. It seemed genuine. Quinn had been wrong about her.

The giant chandelier sparkled at the top of the grand staircase. A few people lounged about in the comfortable lobby chairs. Quinn wondered about them. Why were they all here? Were they just passing through? Quinn searched the faces for Rico and the family with the little girl, but they weren't there. Had they checked out of the hotel like Mr. and Mrs. Cawston? Like Josh? Had they woken up somewhere, somehow, after having been unconscious? Dragged back from the brink of death to live full and happy lives? Quinn hoped so.

She didn't bother looking for Joe or the old man in pajamas, Mr. Mirabelli. Quinn knew they had already taken the elevator ride. Mr. Mirabelli had been waiting—waiting for Jeanette to arrive, whoever that might be. A daughter? A sister? A grandchild? Someone to hold his hand one last time so he could let go. And Joe, he had been waiting for someone to save his brother. Kara had done that. Joe would be happy.

"Are you ready?" said Persephone to the truck driver.

The elevator was waiting. Persephone slid open the metal gate and the man stepped inside. Sharon looked at him and smiled. "All set?" He glanced at Persephone, then at Quinn, and nodded.

Persephone was about to close the metal gate when Quinn had a thought. What if . . . what if he was headed downward? He had done something bad. Would he have to suffer that horrible party for eternity? The image sent shivers parading up her spine.

"Hold on!" she yelled. "Is he—"

"Not for us to say," said Persephone, reading her thoughts.

"But he doesn't deserve it. Not that place."

Persephone looked at Quinn, then at the truck driver. "I'm sure your forgiveness will go a long way."

"Thank you," said the man, tears filling the sad eyes Quinn had once thought were wild and cruel. He looked at Sharon and nodded. "I'm ready."

Sharon winked at the girls and then slid the metal gate closed. She grasped the brass lever. "Fasten your seat belts. We'll be cruising at an altitude of fifty billion feet."

The elevator moved slowly at first. Quinn watched as their heads disappeared. Upward. It was moving upward. Her heart swelled as she leaned in to watch it rise. There was a brilliant flash of glistening light, and then the elevator was gone.

Quinn took a deep breath and sighed. Then she had another thought. She turned toward Persephone. "What about the person who took Emma? Is that person there?" She pointed down the cold dark hollow of the elevator shaft.

Persephone placed a hand on Quinn's shoulder. She shook her head slowly. "Not yet." She smiled and then left the girls standing by the elevator. Someone was waiting for her at the front desk.

Yet, thought Quinn.

Quinn squeezed Emma's hand. "I have so much to tell you."

Emma grinned. "So do I."

Quinn wanted to tell Emma she was sorry, that she loved her, that she missed her and needed her, but all that came out was, "I read the end of your book—*Anne of Avonlea*. Plus a few others from your to-be-read pile."

"Really?" said Emma, her expression a mixture of amusement and surprise. "Will you tell me all about them?"

"Sure," said Quinn, taking her sister's hand. They walked toward the grand staircase. "Let's get you out of this jacket and into a bathing suit. We can hang out at the pool. We'll eat all the hot dogs we want, talk about your books, and even have a swim." She stopped suddenly. "Just watch out for the deep end. It's deeper than you think." She plucked the pink cap from Emma's head and tossed it over her shoulder.

Emma giggled.

As they headed up the steps Quinn saw it—the dark circle around her wrist was returning. She held her sister's hand tightly, but her grasp had weakened. In the distance, she could hear the soft echo of an ambulance siren.

Quinn pulled Emma closer. She talked quickly, buzzing like a wasp, as the two stepped out into the bright sunlight in the courtyard of Inn Between.

Acknowledgments

They say it takes a village to raise a child. The same adage applies to novels. This story would not be what it is today without the help and support of many wonderful people.

A heartfelt thank-you to my first-draft readers, Darlene Beck-Jacobson, Martha Martin, and Jaime Cohen. You lent me your time, provided me with feedback, and kept me moving forward. And Valerie Sherrard, that *little book of positive* sure did the trick.

Thank you to the Ontario Arts Council for your generous support of this work via the Writers' Reserve Program.

A special thank-you to the incredibly talented Sarah Watts for her deliciously creepy cover and illustrations.

To my wonderful children and awesome husband,

Michael Cohen, thank you for putting up with my vacant stares, my three a.m. aha! moments, and the all-too-frequent omelet dinners, and especially for taking care of the endless piles of laundry. You are the reason I write.

John M. Cusick, words are not enough. You plucked my work out of the slush pile, guided me through round after round of cleansing revision, and kept the faith when mine dwindled. You are the best agent ever, a gifted writer, a great mentor, and a good friend. Without you, this story would have been stuck in Inn Between.

And last on this list, but by no means least, the biggest thank-you goes to my genius editor, Emily Feinberg, and everyone at Roaring Brook Press. Connecting with you, Emily, was like finding someone who loves my baby as much as I do. Your keen eyes, brilliant insight, and tireless enthusiasm have made this story sparkle—er, in a dark and creepy way, of course!